THE DISAPPOINTED DIVA

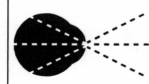

This Large Print Book carries the
Seal of Approval of N.A.V.H.

THE DISAPPOINTED DIVA

EVELYN MINSHULL

THORNDIKE PRESS

An imprint of Thomson Gale, a part of The Thomson Corporation

Detroit • New York • San Francisco • New Haven, Conn. • Waterville, Maine • London

Thorndike Press® Large Print Christian Mystery.
The text of this Large Print edition is unabridged.
Other aspects of the book may vary from the original edition.
Set in 16 pt. Plantin.

LIBRARY OF CONGRESS CATALOGING-IN-PUBLICATION DATA

Minshull, Evelyn White.
    The disappointed diva : church choir mysteries / by Evelyn Minshull.
        p. cm. — (Thorndike Press large print Christian mystery)
    ISBN-13: 978-0-7862-9924-9 (hardcover : alk. paper)
    ISBN-10: 978-0-7862-9924-X (hardcover : alk. paper)
    1. Women singers — Fiction. 2. Choirs (Music) — Fiction. 3. Cats —
Fiction. 4. Large type books. I. Title.
PS3563.I476D57 2007
813'.54—dc22   2007030038

Published in 2007 by arrangement with Guideposts a Church Corporation.

Printed in the United States of America on permanent paper
10 9 8 7 6 5 4 3 2 1

For the Getschmans
— Pastor Bob and Goldye —
for introducing our women's group
to the baby-shower-by-proxy.

ACKNOWLEDGMENTS

A standing ovation — complete with confetti — for the trio at Guideposts Books & Inspirational Media Division for their guidance, nurturing and gentle suggestions. Thanks, Elizabeth Kramer Gold, Michele Slung and Stephanie Castillo Samoy!

1

"I am arrive!"

The new choir member who burst through the sanctuary door of Eternal Hope Community Church on a blast of frigid December air was as theatrical in appearance as in entrance. Her abundant dark hair towered in coils that increased her already impressive height. There in the scant light, the galaxies of sequins on her scarf sparked like heat lightning. Her crimson cloak — capacious enough to enclose the entire Eternal Hope soprano section, except, perhaps, for Estelle Livett — ballooned as she swept into a dramatic bow. "I, Maria Carlotta Estalena Lucia Buonarotti, am delighted to join your splendid cantata!"

Gracie Lynn Parks had never before seen her fellow choir members so immobilized. Marge Lawrence, Gracie's best friend and nearest neighbor, who was usually so voluble, managed only a few startled gasps.

Choir director Barb Jennings seemed momentarily incapable of controlling her baton — the ultimate symbol of authority, Gracie sometimes felt, in all of Willow Bend, Indiana. Even Estelle Livett toned down her coloratura vocalizing in obedience to a flick of that slender scepter. Sometimes, anyway.

But in the overwhelming presence of Maria Carlotta Estalena Lucia Buonarotti, both the baton and its wielder seemed powerless.

As did the remainder of the choir.

Gracie was the first to recover. "Do come up!" She gestured toward a pew cluttered with a hodgepodge of winter wraps. "You could leave your — *uh* — cape there, if you like."

Instead, Maria surveyed the choir. "The soprano section is, I believe," she pointed, "right here?" Not waiting for response, she nodded. "Of course. It is always so, even in the operatic choruses — even in Italy."

Gasping, Estelle Livett sank back into her chair.

Amy Cantrell slipped from her place, descended the steps with quick grace, and took the newcomer's elbow. "You can stand right by me," the blond teenager said. "We can share music. Is that all right with you?"

Maria nodded imperiously.

Estelle groaned.

Give her credit, though, Lord, Gracie prayed silently. *She's masking it well.* Gracie suspected that *it* was a fear of being displaced as Eternal Hope's diva, a self-appointed position. She was, as Estelle reminded them at every opportunity, the only female choir member with genuine musical training.

Gracie herself looked forward to the injection of fresh energy this flamboyant woman might offer. *You have a way, Lord, of blending unlikely ingredients for maximum effect.*

This happy mixture constantly occurred in nature, where dandelions co-exist with rare exotics. It also characterized Gracie's creative catering — an unexpected dash of cumin here, a sprinkling of rosemary there. Certainly, to date, each added voice had further enriched the choir of Eternal Hope Community Church, even if only temporarily.

"Well, then," Barb said at last. She raised her baton, throats cleared, and each section found its beginning note.

For centuries they'd waited,
Watched and waited,
Prayed and waited —
Crying for a Savior
Who would heal their nation's pain.

11

For centuries they'd prayed for Him,
Watched and sighed and prayed for Him,
Yearning for this Savior
Who would make them strong again.

If they had expected an opera singer to dominate, they were pleasantly surprised. Maria's mellow notes — pure, crystalline, unassuming — soared with the sopranos. Then, when balance faltered, they dropped to contralto, tenor, even bass.

Like binder, Gracie thought, she's an adhesive, like that keystone on which a structure rests.

Lord, thank You! Before, we were a patchwork quilt. Now we more resemble a tapestry!

"Maria," Barb suggested softly, "could you manage an obligato here?"

God promised them a Savior,
And they knew that God is true —
That what God said He'd bring to pass
He certainly would do.
And yet the time grew very long.
They heard the groaning, not the song.
Throughout the fear, the chilling fear,
They prayed the Savior might appear
To bring them safety,
Teach them gladness,
Show them peace

And end their sadness
And so they waited . . . waited . . . waited
And so they watched and prayed.
Perhaps He'd come . . .
Today!

The last phrase died off, followed by a silence so intense, so breathless, that Gracie imagined hearing the rhythms of many hearts, beating as one.

They had practiced this song before — perhaps a dozen times — and after their first tentative run-throughs it had "worked."

But never like this, never soaring so gloriously! Gracie wondered if even the angels in heaven might listen in — and smile.

The silence continued, then became a stirring. Gracie smiled to herself. The mind and the soul might remain captive, but stiff muscles, after all, required stretching.

"That was wonderful!" Comfort Harding, clutching her daughter Lillian's little hand, tiptoed from the room where the congregation's smallest children had been practicing their pageant.

Lillian giggled as she saw her father, a handsome African American adored by his fellow choir members for his generosity of spirit, and also for his supple tenor.

What a blessing he's been, Lord! Gracie

thought. Except for Estelle — and now Maria — Rick Harding was the only member of the choir who came with "credentials."

"I'm here!" Lillian sang out, and the other children crowded close behind.

"If you're ready, so are we!" Barb turned to the third song in the cantata booklet. " 'Clouds,' " she said, and pages riffled.

"Shepherds first." Comfort herded a bevy of boys clad in striped bathrobes.

Estelle muttered, "Isn't it about time we got some real costumes?"

Barb said crisply, "I imagine these robes would have looked rather good to the original shepherds."

"Moth-eaten —" Estelle pursued.

"But not flea-bitten or burr-encrusted."

"And not smelling of sweat —" Tyne Anderson contributed.

"— nor sheep dung," her twin sister Tish Ball completed her thought. The Turner twins had done this trick all their lives.

Estelle shuddered delicately. "Please!"

"Ever been to a sheep pen?" Don Delano, who taught high school science, chuckled.

But Gracie's attention had fallen elsewhere.

The children — all but one — were wiggling, grinning widely, obviously impatient to perform their parts.

14

But Patsy Clayton, leaning on her walker, seemed close to tears.

Oh, my, Gracie wondered, what could have happened to dim her enthusiasm for Christmas? In other years, this blessed child had been among the most enthusiastic.

The shepherds were in position. Barb tapped her baton. "Remember the wonder! The hush! The fear! Softly, but with expression!"

They looked like clouds at first, above us,
As we rested on the ground —
Moving as clouds often travel.
　　Then came the sound.
I had seen bright stars and moonglow
Lighting mountains and abyss,
But in all my years as shepherd —
　　Nothing like this!
I had heard the songs of tempests
And the breeze's gentle sighs
But I'd never heard such music
　　As from these skies!

Gracie loved the song. It was positively thrilling to hear Rick's expressive tenor and Maria's rich contralto. She exulted in the phrases where her own section, the altos, assumed the melody.

But her attention was soon divided between the wonderful story unfolding in song and action and Patsy, slumping in a pew.

> Trembling knees collapsed me earthward,
> But my soul, expanded, stirred —
> For I sensed the age-old promise
>   Found in God's Word.
> "Fear ye not," the angels urged us,
> And my fear dissolved like dew.
> "For we bring a holy message
>   Of joy to you —"

Patsy had disappeared.

Lord, what's happened? Is Patsy facing a new medical ordeal? Is she in pain? Please touch her heart with additional love. And make sure, please, I know as quickly as possible what's troubling her.

2

"I'm worried about Patsy."

Uncle Miltie dipped a spoon into his dish of pistachio ice cream. "What is there about this season?" He sighed. "First Abe. Now that sweet child."

"Abe?" Gracie's own spoon paused. Abe Wasserman, the local deli owner, was one of their dearest friends.

"Well, not Abe himself." Uncle Miltie savored a large, slow bite before saying, "Sophie."

Sophie Glass, Abe's sister, maintained a sort of dual citizenship in Florida and Willow Bend. At the moment she was visiting Abe for Hanukkah, and Willow Bend rejoiced. Sophie's baking skills were legendary, and her blintzes a peak achievement.

"She isn't ill, is she?"

"Not that I know." Another bite. "At least not physically." Another spoonful. *"Yum."*

Gracie felt a strong urge to hold her

uncle's spoon still until she'd forced him to tell her what he knew.

"Then what? Mentally?" she challenged. It seemed unlikely. Her friend's sister could be strong-willed, perhaps on occasion even excessively bossy. Sophie would never be truly content until she had drawn Abe to Florida — a move he resisted mightily.

In that regard, Gracie was on his side.

"Hard to say," Uncle Miltie continued. "She was preoccupied, Abe said. Secretive. Sometimes she was humming and grinning, and minutes later, she seemed to have descended into the Slough of Despond." He winked. "Bet you didn't think I'd remember 'The Rime of the Ancient Mariner,' did you?"

"Pilgrim's Progress," she corrected absently. *Lord, he's describing manic-depression, isn't he? But how is that possible? There's never been any sign —*

Or had there? Had she been so busy with her own affairs that she'd failed to notice?

"So what's up with Patsy?" Uncle Miltie asked.

She sighed. "I wish I knew. I'd hoped to see her after choir practice, when she seemed so upset — but she was already gone."

He patted her hand. "You can't solve

everyone's problems, my dear, no matter how hard you try. But, knowing you, you'll stretch your morning praise-walk tomorrow to indulge a visit to both Sophie and Patsy. Now go on and eat your ice cream, like a good girl, and listen to a new joke of mine."

She groaned — since it was obligatory — then grinned.

"Now, now, none of that. This is one of my better ones!"

She grinned again. "I can't wait."

"Nor will you have to, dear girl." He scooped up the last of his ice cream and thoroughly licked the spoon. "Why did the frog mechanic go to the hardware store?"

She had no idea. "He needed more rib-bits?" she guessed wildly, then waited for his exultant chortle and the "real" answer.

Instead, he looked totally desolate. "You already heard it."

"No, I promise I hadn't." She patted his arm. "Oh, Uncle Miltie, I'm so sorry! It just seemed — rivets, ribbits — I was only guessing!"

"Maybe I'm losing my touch," he murmured.

"No! Never! It was great! See me laugh!"

She threw her head back and gave an emphatic chuckle. *Ho, ho!* She looked at him. "How's that?"

He shook his head.

"Well, then, you can't help it if you have a brilliant niece," she teased him.

He gave her an unconvincing smile in return. "Let me take your bowl, if you're finished. I can still rinse dishes, at least."

Do me a favor, Lord — please?

Since the morning was brisk, she had decided to prayer-walk to a Christian rock tape. Gooseberry, her large orange cat, scurried ahead. Apparently he had spotted a brilliant cardinal, confidently worrying a cluster of dogwood berries.

She paused in her conversation with the Lord until she was certain the cardinal was safe. Gooseberry, unchastened by the bird's tongue-lashing, pranced off, with his tail proudly aloft, in search of more cooperative prey.

It's this, Lord. Help me to approach Patsy — and Sophie, too — without looking like some inquisitive busybody. It's just that I care about them both so much! Give me the words — the words of caring, of sharing, of healing. It doesn't matter if I solve the problems at hand — all I ask is to be a conduit for Your love.

She switched off the tape. She preferred quiet when she expected Him to guide her.

Even He might have trouble competing with steel drums, electric guitars amped to the max and vocals operating on the concept that volume covers a multitude of musical sins.

She breathed in the lung-scraping cold. How fresh the air was, flavored with pine scent and woodsmoke! So far this winter, snow had been scarce, but last night's wind had driven icy pellets into the crevices of fissured sassafras bark, coated pine and hemlock needles, and edged with white the stubborn, brittle leaves of oaks.

From the scent of the breeze and the smudged clouds, more snow was on the way. But that was fine with Gracie. There would be snow for the weeks preceding Christmas!

Comfort Harding, juggling a jumble of wires and plump green gardenias, called out a greeting. Lillian, bundled up with only her tiny face visible, held aloft a mittened hand, waving slowly, hampered by the roly-poly bulk of her snowsuit.

Gracie walked over. "May I help?" She admired the Hardings' Christmas decorations.

"Thanks! If you could hold the end of the garland, just until I get it secure —"

She had woven large red holly berries into

the gleaming green.

"It's lovely!" Gracie said.

"It's going to be lopsided!" Comfort stood back, surveying her handiwork. Then she shrugged and said, "But what does it matter? If it were perfectly adjusted, it would be out of sync with the occupants of the house! Thanks for coming to my rescue! Could I return the favor with a cup of chocolate?"

Gracie hesitated. Not that she truly worried about her weight — she was, after all, a cook who enjoyed her own culinary creations — but calories were always out there waiting to ambush you. Her talks with God were, of course, fat-free, loaded with wonderful spiritual nutrition.

On the other hand, Comfort, who worked at Keefer Memorial Hospital, might be able to shed some light on Patsy's melancholy.

"I accept!" She followed Comfort into the warm house, while the muffled Lillian — impervious to harm — tumbled about the porch.

"Let me take your jacket and scarf — and make yourself at home. Or, 'Make yourself homely,' as your uncle might say! Not that you could be, Gracie!"

They both laughed.

Comfort had recently redone the Hardings' kitchen in a rooster theme. Around them Gracie saw colorful ceramics, a fabric hanging, painted iron trivets, a comical cookie jar and a wall clock, all featuring roosters.

"Nothing like jumping on the bandwagon when the parade's past!" Comfort set a teakettle on the gas stove's front burner. "Roosters were big — when? A year or so ago?" She reached for rooster mugs, handing one to Gracie.

"Does it really matter?" Careful not to spill anything, Gracie turned the rooster salt and pepper shakers over in her hands. "As long as they make you happy!"

"You're right, as always. And I got lucky at a rummage sale a couple of weekends ago. The owner must have been moving on to some new animal!"

The hot chocolate was soul-satisfying as only something warm and sweet can be. Gracie inhaled, enjoying the lovely wintertime sensation. Hot chocolate in the summer was hardly the same.

Comfort produced a plate of lemon crescents, covered with confectioner's sugar.

"Guaranteed sugar-free!" Comfort leaned her elbows on the table, her slim brown hands cupping her steaming mug.

"Well, then." Gracie accepted a cookie and nibbled a point. "Wonderful! Your own recipe?"

"I wish! I bought them at the Deli."

Sophie!

"Did you see . . . anyone besides Abe?"

Comfort frowned thoughtfully. "Pastor Paul was having pancakes. It really isn't fair, is it, that men can eat anything they want and never gain an ounce?" She took a sip of chocolate. "That pretty activities director from Pleasant Haven was with him. She was having an unbuttered bagel and plain tea. She couldn't take her eyes from his pancakes, but he never offered her a bite, just went on and on about how delicious they were." She giggled. "For such a gifted pastor and sweet man, he has some blind spots, doesn't he?"

Gracie nodded. "He seems to have no idea how attractive he is. Half the female members of Eternal Hope think he's the best thing since sliced bread — but he's pretty clueless."

"I keep waiting to see who'll snag him."

"Maybe no one will. When he's seventy and still our pastor, he may wake up one morning, look around and remember eating breakfast with Blaise Bloomfield!"

They looked at one another. "Men!" they exclaimed affectionately in unison.

"Oh, and speaking of romance —" Comfort teased. "Rocky was there, too. At the Deli."

Gracie felt her face warming. Rocco Gravino, editor and publisher of the *Mason County Gazette,* was certainly the best male companion Gracie knew. Until her own Elmo's untimely death, the two men had been close friends.

Comfort said, "Probably as many people wonder about you and Rocky as about Pastor Paul."

Gracie took a bite of lemon crescent. "We're just good friends." She licked a smidgeon of powdered sugar off her fingertip. "*Hmm.* Good."

Comfort merely winked in reply.

It's time to get the conversation back on track, Gracie decided. "Then you didn't see Sophie?"

"No. I heard her, though, back in the kitchen, singing and banging pots and pans." She frowned. "She sounded happy, but Abe kept glancing toward the kitchen. Something about her definitely concerns him."

Gracie thought about this as they finished their chocolate. She declined seconds.

She hadn't yet asked about Patsy.

"Gracie." Comfort turned from the dishwasher, one mug still in her hand. She hesitated. "I wonder if you'd . . . talk to Patsy Clayton."

Gracie's heart jolted. "So you noticed, too."

"It would be impossible not to! Last night when anyone tried to talk with her, to draw her into the excitement, her eyes filled with tears. She seemed to *want* to talk — I think she just couldn't, at least not without crying." Comfort sighed. "I don't like it. What if they've found there's nothing they can do for her — not even with further surgery?" She clutched the drainboard. Comfort was a doctor, it was true, but she was a woman and mother in her heart.

"Gracie — what if that sweet little girl is . . . *dying?*"

3

Gracie's stride was less buoyant as she continued her walk. It wasn't the hot chocolate and cookies weighing her down — well, at least not totally — it was the dread stirred up by Comfort's disturbing question.

Children did die. Everyone realized that, and grieved deeply at each young passing — for the loss of potential, of innocence, of sweetness.

Lord, we can't begin to understand Your ways — only trust that the little ones who leave this earth before they've fully experienced it are delighted with Your much better world. But what a hole is left in our hearts!

She couldn't imagine Willow Bend without Patsy Clayton. The landscape was enriched by her holding a place in it, and the wheelchair she frequently used trailed valiant purple streamers behind. She was a merry little girl, and a brave one, her staunchness and good cheer a banner to one and all, just like those purple ribbons.

A sense of peace eased into Gracie's heart. She slowed down even more. Gooseberry meowed a protest and strode off on his own, but Gracie scarcely noticed.

It was as if a certainty had settled within her mind and spirit. Patsy *wasn't* dying. Praise the Lord!

But please help me to deal with her problem — whatever it is. I know that You're already working in her heart.

Patsy loves You, Lord — more purely, more joyously than any adult I know —

She straightened her shoulders and marched on. She and the Lord were in this together. No problem was too big!

Amy Cantrell — her blue fleece parka open, revealing a waitress uniform — called out a greeting. "Come help, Gracie! Abe will be sending out the National Guard to track me down — but how can we leave Horace headless?"

Horace, Gracie saw, was a somewhat hapless snowman. Gracie wondered how Amy and Patsy had gathered enough snow for even such a small one.

Amy, who lived next door to Patsy, could have been a poster girl for glowing good health. With her cheeks rosy from the cold and her blue eyes sparkling, she looked vibrantly alive.

Patsy presented a marked contrast. Though the chill had brightened her nose and cheeks, as well, her eyes and posture spoke listlessness as she kicked idly at Horace's base, threatening his already tenuous hold on gravity. "It was a dumb idea, anyway. I mean, anyone can see there's not enough snow —"

She broke off, and Gracie sensed she was holding back tears. Gracie and Amy exchanged glances.

Amy sighed. "I really have to get to work —"

"I'll stay and visit for a while, then!" Gracie forced her voice to a brightness she didn't feel. "We can either finish Horace — I'm certain we can manage to scrape up a bit more snow somewhere — or else we can sit on the porch steps and talk."

Patsy made no comment, only dragged the toe of one bright yellow boot along the ground. Purring loudly, Gooseberry wound around her ankles, but she took no notice even of him.

Refusing to be rebuffed, he stalked off to converse with a neighbor's cat-friendly mutt. While Marge's Shih Tzu Charlotte, Gooseberry's best friend, was every furry

29

inch a blueblood, Gracie's pet was eclectic in his friendships. "Not a smobbish whisker on his face!" Uncle Miltie was fond of saying. "My kind of cat."

Amy was nearly out of sight, and although she was fairly jogging in her hurry to reach work on time, Gracie knew her well enough to suspect that her thoughts were lingering on her troubled young friend.

"Which would you rather, Patsy? Finish Horace or have me just visit?"

Patsy shrugged.

What now, Lord?

Then, in a whisper, Patsy said, "Snowmen are a big waste of time. Everything's a waste of time!"

Gracie's heart sank.

"Actually. . . ." Patsy's mittened hand slipped into Gracie's. "Actually, I really do need to talk."

Thank You, Lord!

"But —" Patsy looked around almost furtively. "Could we go to your place, do you s'pose?"

"Of course! But I wonder — are cookies a waste of time, too?"

Patsy managed a small giggle.

"Then let your mother know where we're off to. I've always found that cookies and conversation go very well together!"

A visit with Sophie, and finishing her walk, would just have to wait.

They headed down the street slowly, Patsy scuffing her boots and walker in the thin snow.

"Even Christmas decorations," Patsy grumbled, "are a waste of time. 'Specially when they get broke or stolen."

"Did someone break or steal some of your family's?" Gracie was saddened but not shocked. Even Willow Bend had trouble-makers.

"Mrs. Cooper's. It was a Grinch. A limb fell and cracked off his arm. And then — when Mrs. Cooper's son went out to get it to fix, he was gone."

Gracie couldn't help frowning. She hated to think of thievery in her beloved Willow Bend. But before she could offer some alternative possibility, Patsy continued.

"And there are others, too. A giant candy cane, two doors up. A truck backed into it, I think. And an elf. I don't know how it got broke."

"Then they were stolen, too?" Gracie asked.

Patsy nodded. "So what's the use? It's all a big waste of time!"

Gooseberry was already home, having

recognized a faltering in Gracie's dedication to exercise. Human relations weren't his thing, except when they related to him. He was curled up on the couch with Uncle Miltie and a bowl of potato chips. A rerun of a *Bonanza* episode ran with muted sound.

"Gooseberry and I are practicing our lip-reading." Uncle Miltie swung his legs to the floor. "Nellie Stover" — she was the principal of the local elementary school — "wants me to talk about signing to some classes the first of the year, when nobody's quite ready to get back to real work."

Gracie patted his shoulder, then hung her jacket and Patsy's over chairs to dry.

Patsy set her wet mittens by the rim of the sink. "What are they saying now, Mr. Morgan?"

Gracie was pleased to note the child's sudden interest.

Uncle Miltie frowned in concentration. "I think Hoss Cartwright just asked for one of our potato chips!"

Patsy giggled. "You're funny, Mr. Morgan."

He set aside the bowl and leaned forward. "Why did the tired-out rabbit go to the grain store?"

Patsy considered. "Would they have carrots there?"

"No."

"Or lettuce?"

"Give up?"

Patsy shook her head. "Parsley's an herb — isn't it, Mrs. Parks?"

Uncle Miltie cleared his throat. "You want to try, Gracie?"

If there were such a thing as a tentative challenge, Gracie decided, this was it. There was no way she'd take a chance on ruining another riddle for him!

"We give up," Patsy said, as Gracie shook her head.

Uncle Miltie chuckled. "The tired rabbit went to find some hops!"

"It must be fun living with your uncle," Patsy said later. She looked at Gracie wistfully. "Nobody could be sad around him." She had a streak of flour on her cheek, which she rubbed at absently.

Gracie set a pan of chocolate drop cookies on the oven's middle rack and eased shut the door. It was difficult *not* to ask what was troubling her — but she had determined to give Patsy all the space she needed.

"I never used to be sad." Her voice dropped to a murmur. "Now, I'm hardly ever *not* sad!"

Gracie perched on a stool and waited. She

idly reached for a catalogue that lay nearby.

"It's just . . . losing a friend is really hard!"

"Yes it is, dear." Gracie thrashed about in her mind for someone Patsy might mean. She couldn't think of anyone Patsy's age who had moved away, or a relative — even one at a distance — who had recently died. In a town as small as Willow Bend, such events were common knowledge.

"But I just don't believe anymore."

Gracie felt a chill in her heart.

"Believe . . . ?" she ventured.

Patsy sighed deeply, elbows propped on the table, her chin resting in her hands. "How can I, Mrs. Parks? I've prayed and prayed and prayed — and so has everyone I know. But none of the operations help, and the doctors just shake their heads. If God was real, I mean if He really *cared* — then don't you think He'd listen?"

"Oh, Patsy dear!" Gracie gathered the child in her arms, but Patsy — with a strength that surprised Gracie — pulled away.

"And so I've made up my mind. There isn't any God. But oh, Mrs. Parks —" Her face crumpled, and she put her tear-wet cheek close to Gracie's. "You can't believe how much I miss Him!"

4

Pastor Paul Meyer frowned. "That's a tough one, Gracie! We're told 'Ask and ye shall receive.' So how do we explain to a child who has asked and asked . . . and *asked* that sometimes God's answer is 'No' — and that ultimately we will discover it the best possible response?"

Rocky gave a mild snort scarcely audible against the background of voices, clinking china, the ding of the cash register and Sophie's tuneless singing in the kitchen.

Pastor Paul raised a questioning eyebrow. "The editor disagrees?"

"Firmly." Rocky paused while Amy distributed menus and recited the day's specials — chili with homemade garlic bread, vegetable quiche or pot roast.

When they had made their choices, Rocky continued. "How can you tell a woman who's lost her husband and only son to a drunk driver that everything's for the best?

Think someday she'll come to agree, finally, that it was the right thing that they died like that?"

Pastor Paul said mildly, "God didn't choreograph the accident."

"He allowed it to happen!"

"He gives us free will. He won't step in and arbitrarily cancel the gift."

"Why not? If He's God?"

"Because then He'd be as capricious as Zeus on Mount Olympus. Or — perhaps even worse — a puppet-master, jerking us around at will — whether or not we agree. Like any good father, He first gives us direction, then grants the freedom to make our own mistakes — and learn from them."

"The bereaved wife and mother might find *that* 'capricious.' She might assume that a responsible parent would restrain an unruly child — especially one heedless of the safety of others."

Unfolding his napkin, Pastor Paul admitted, "No doubt, at first, she'd be furious with God for not intervening. But later —"

"She'd accept the belief that they're in heaven — and she should be grateful — even though there's no money for her rent and groceries? Even though she's so lonely she cries herself to sleep every night? Rather meager comfort, my friend, don't you think?"

Gracie winced. She knew that Pastor Paul and Rocky respected one another. She understood that while they found their verbal sparring energizing, both realized that the chance of their ever agreeing on spiritual matters was slim indeed.

But there was an unaccustomed edge to Rocky's voice this time, and it wounded her spirit.

Lord, will this dear friend of mine — of ours — ever come to a true knowledge of You? How she yearned for that!

Delivering their drinks and salads, Amy set a pitcher of clinking ice water on the red formica tabletop. As soon as she walked away, Rocky pressed his attack. "So let me get this straight. You're suggesting that God *did* 'choreograph' Patsy's problems?"

"Not at all."

Rocky said, "Then God doesn't take responsibility for anything? Except the good stuff, of course. He gets the credit for Creation, medical miracles, scientific discoveries, all that." He speared a dill pickle and glared at it. "If a news story gets skewed, I'm held accountable. If Abe runs out of coffee, he takes the flak. But God —"

Pastor Paul intervened smoothly, "I'm

delighted, my editorial friend! At last we agree that God exists!"

Rocky's instant sputtering was interrupted by the arrival of their dinners.

With the aroma of the juicy pot roast Pastor Paul had ordered distracting them, Gracie spoke for the table. "*Mmm.* God is good!"

Even Rocky had the grace to chuckle.

Forgive me, Lord, for injecting my own bit of mischief into the mix — but laughter is surely better for the digestion than conflict!

Joining hands, they bowed their heads while Pastor Paul thanked God properly for the meal they were about to enjoy.

It wasn't until their table was cleared, except for coffee refills, that Abe found time to join them. He carried his own steaming mug. Rocky shifted closer to Gracie in the booth to allow more room.

"I have been a poor host." He signaled Amy, who appeared immediately with a platter of fruit-filled pastries. "My treat."

"Apology accepted!" Rocky eyed the tray, but passed it first to Gracie.

She selected one oozing apricot juice. The rugelach was browned to a golden perfection. "Sophie," she sighed, "is a genius!"

"So I tell her." Abe beamed. "And sometimes she even believes me!"

Gracie glanced toward the kitchen, which was nearly silent, now. The dishwasher hummed, a garbage disposal growled. But there were no *"la-la-la's"* to signal Sophie's presence.

Abe answered her questioning look. "Gone home," he said. "She was expecting a call. Some Florida friend, I think." He gazed up from under his salt-and-pepper eyebrows at his companions.

"It seemed you were having a heavy discussion. Was it about the fate of civilization as we know it? Or merely the poor varsity football season? I feel quite sure it couldn't have been anything like the way God works in our lives. . . ."

Rocky snorted again.

Pastor Paul answered diplomatically. "Our dinners arrived, and we forgot the topics that had been giving us occasion to disagree!"

Gracie sighed happily. What a good man he was! What good friends these were! And what good food Abe served!

"That reminds me. I have a call coming, too — about a reception I'll be catering." She leaned to kiss Abe's cheek. "I'm sorry to leave, when you just got here."

"One kiss from such a charming redhead

and I forgive anything. But first —" He caught her arm. "Estelle was in this afternoon, and . . . do you have any idea what might be troubling her?"

Gracie sank back into her seat.

5

Abe admitted, "I might not have noticed her preoccupation, but Sophie's been moody lately, too."

Paul nodded. "Depression's not unusual during holidays."

Gracie and Elmo had often spoken of this — that no family gathering ever achieves the perfection depicted in Norman Rockwell paintings or any of the thousands of holiday ads. The reality is that squabbles, sulks, weariness, clamor and culinary crises result in disappointment, guilt — and often despair.

Especially for people without God.

But Estelle had God.

Even so, her always tenuous self-confidence was tottering in the presence of newcomer Maria Carlotta Estalena Lucia Buonarotti's superior talent.

Lord, is this something I should share? Or is Estelle's jealous pique something she should be allowed to work out in private? Yet Abe cares or he wouldn't ask. . . .

Her answer came in the concerned expressions of all three of the men sitting with her.

"You know, don't you, Gracie?" Abe's voice was gentle but expectant.

She nodded.

And told them.

When the explanation had been given, there was silence.

"I know," she said. "I feel helpless, too." In fact, helplessness seemed to be the order of the day. "Estelle can be so . . . bristly. Whatever we might say to comfort her always has a ninety-five percent chance of being misconstrued."

Pastor Paul nodded. "And then she's more hurt than before. And yet. . . ."

"And yet," Abe repeated, leaned back in his chair and smiled.

"Oh, oh," Rocky warned. "I feel a story coming!" He grinned. "I need fortification. Pass the rugelach, please?" He took his fourth raspberry-filled one.

Abe lifted his mug as a signal to Amy, and she brought the carafe to give everyone refills.

She looked patient, Gracie thought, but

there were still tables to be cleaned, sugar bowls and salt and pepper shakers to fill. And there they were, sitting and showing signs of being happily settled for some time to come. Amy's sweet expression showed she didn't regard her part-time job as drudgery.

"Sit down, sweet Amy," Abe invited. He pulled over an extra chair for her, like the affectionate employer he was.

Setting the tray she was carrying on a nearby table, she nestled gratefully into the seat, waiting for Abe to begin. His stories never failed to surprise, and their settings were often exotic.

"There came a day when the animals of the jungle assembled to receive their voices," he began. "It was a beautiful day, sun-swept and breezy, with swaying tan grasses and tossing tropical foliage. Pale orchids clustered in luminous constellations. Brilliant birds — macaws, toucans, cockatoos — carried their colors like banners from high limb to high limb. But as yet no birdsongs gladdened the ear. No panther kittens meowed, no hyena pups yipped, no monkeys chattered, screeched or scolded.

"They met in a clearing near a broad river. A large basket woven of reeds held hundreds of small bundles. The voices. Expectancy throbbed. And yes, fear — for each wanted his voice to command respect, even admiration.

"No one was more nervous than Frog — since his would be the voice that ruled the ponds and streams. For obvious reasons, Fish was unable to attend, and Crayfish — content to scuttle forwards, backwards and sideways, raising small, dark clouds of silt — had declined the invitation.

"One by one, the jungle's inhabitants received their voices. Immediately, each tried his out. Many voices were serviceable, Frog supposed, but he was happy he hadn't received the bugling sound of Water Buffalo, or the silly cackling of Parrot. The best ones were being saved for last, it seemed. While Frog waited his turn, he tried to imagine which sound would be his. But it wasn't until the smaller birds flourished their songs that he began to feel envy. Oh, to speak so musically! Surely his voice would be at least as fine as theirs!" Here, Abe glanced around and smiled.

"His envy grew when he heard the sound given to Lion, a lilting, silvery, rippling voice that belonged in ponds or rivers — not stuck on the savannahs or off in rocky shelter.

"Even before Frog received his own

packet, he knew that he would hate his voice. Nevertheless, he tried it. It was worse than he had imagined! It had no panache whatsoever! When he gave it full volume, it roared alarmingly — causing monkeys and birds to shriek high into the vine-laden trees — the smaller animals shrinking into shadows or streaking to some place of hiding. He hated it! He didn't want to frighten, he yearned to enchant. To delight." Abe raised an expressive eyebrow.

"What he truly desired was the voice given to Lion. Surely, he thought, there had been a terrible mistake. The more he entertained the possibility, the more certain he became. His voice had been given to Lion in error."

Abe took a long sip of coffee — no longer steaming. He sighed.

Rocky cleared his throat in warning. "If this is another —"

"Ah, no, my friend! This story does indeed have an ending."

Stirring uneasily, Amy glanced around at work still undone.

Abe patted her arm. "I'll help finish with cleanup."

"Oh, good! Because you haven't gotten to Estelle yet!"

Abe threw back his head in a great guffaw.

Pastor Paul said gently, "I think he may have, Amy."

Estelle, Gracie feared, would scarcely appreciate the amphibian analogy. A frog!

"Did I not say 'he?' " Abe asked innocently. "I was certain I said 'he.' " He looked about the small circle for confirmation.

Heads nodded, and he resumed his story.

"The plan evolved slowly. As intent as Frog was on his mission, he was acutely aware of Lion's impressive teeth. It would be prudent, he decided, to wait until night, when Lion was soundly asleep. No need to talk things over, he would simply take what was rightfully his and lose himself in the darkness.

"He waited through the long, hot afternoon . . . through that brilliant hour when the sun slips into scarlet and gold . . . past the time when the moon overlaid the jungle with silver . . . until the world was all but silent in cloud-covered darkness.

"We will not belabor the dangers of his journey, how often he tangled in unseen vines, how many tree trunks bruised him . . . how his poor webbed feet suffered on the sharp rocks leading to the cave where Lion snored in ripples and runs of beautiful notes. Frog paused to listen. Soon, he thought, soon that will be my snoring! In and out went the glorious voice. Frog braced himself. He would have one chance, and one only. As Lion breathed out in a great explosion of song, quickly, Frog captured it, taking it as his own. Then, to be fair, he released his rumbling voice from its packet and placed it near Lion's nose — uncomfortably close to those sharp teeth. Backing away, Frog knew he had been successful. Lion was snoring mellow, rumbling notes — and when he coughed, the sound came out in a short, barking roar.

"Quickly, scuttling, Frog jump-hopped in great leapings. Landings jolted the breath from him — startling short bursts of his new song — his ears always alert in case he were followed or otherwise discovered."

Again, Abe paused. Amy tried — without success — to stifle a yawn. Rocky peered into his long-empty mug — as though, miraculously, it might have filled itself since the last time he looked.

"At length, on his large green pad in the center of his pond, Frog luxuriated in his stolen treasure. Experimenting, he exulted in exquisite runs and trills, in warblings that softened to lullaby status, then swelled until the world reverberated with melody. But as night succumbed to slow dawning, Frog

47

became fearful. Everyone would recognize that his voice had first been given to Lion — accidentally, of course, but only Frog knew that. How they would scorn him! Lion might perhaps try to retrieve what had been given him. Frog shuddered, remembering those awesome teeth. But — teeth or no — Frog would not surrender his fabulous voice!

"Perhaps if he hid it for a time — until everyone forgot. Yes! That was the answer! Wrapping it in its packet, he plunged deep into the pond and placed it in silt, then covered it with a clam shell and weighted it with small rocks. It would be safe there! He would go voiceless until it was safe to bring it out. All that day and the next he hopped about, eavesdropping, but hearing no mention of the theft. All of the creatures were so enamored with their own voices that they had no time for gossip.

"But perhaps they were only hoping to trick him into revealing his hiding place! No. He would leave the packet hidden a bit longer. Orchids bloomed and faded. Python shed his old skin and left it hanging from a vine. Parrot's eggs hatched, and the babies feathered, grew and took flight. Lion played with a litter of cubs, taught hunting skills — and, finally, Frog believed himself safe. One early morning he dove deep into the pond, found the rocks, the shell, the silt and the packet — which by now was a bit ragged and discolored. His heart nearly burst with joy at thought of the songs he would sing, the admiring — even envious — glances he would receive. Many animals had arrived at the pond to drink. They conversed quietly in their grunts and barks and chirps. Their various voices combined in a pleasant chorus, and — eagerly — Frog opened his mouth to let out his thrilling song.

" 'Crooo-aaa-kkkk!' "

"The other animals looked up, startled, water dripping from their muzzles or beaks.

"Frog tried again . . . and again . . . and again. Joining the group, Lion seemed to be smiling. His mouth opened just enough to show those alarming teeth, and he gave a mellow roar. He seemed quite content as smaller animals shrank or scuttled away. He lay down, massive head on his paws, and seemed to wait for Frog to sing again. Again came that horrible rasping sound.

"Surely, once it dries out, Frog thought, it will be beautiful once more. But his voice — grown rusty from its long confinement in water — never reclaimed its beauty — even until today."

"Hmm," Pastor Paul commented.

49

Abe reminded him, "It's a fable, my friend."

Pastor Paul smiled. "The message is one I often preach — Be content with who you are. Praise God for the gifts and opportunities you have been given, since He has created them to 'fit' only you."

"Does this mean," Rocky asked innocently, "that I should no longer covet a Pulitzer?"

Amy stood, stretching. "That isn't coveting. That's . . . that's —" She yawned.

"Motivation," Gracie said. "Being the best you can be. God encourages that."

As Amy looked to her minister for confirmation, Gracie thought of Estelle. She was neither lion nor frog, merely one of God's children with a strong desire to shine in His light. Her little vanities could be annoying, but her heart was in the right place, and, really, no one could ever accuse her of croaking.

6

Gracie was up before five, after an all-but-sleepless night. Gooseberry, having retreated to the edge of the bed, presented a study in relaxed contentment. Brilliant as he was, he didn't realize that he should be worrying about Estelle Livett, Patsy Clayton and an imminent catering event for which little had so far been done.

Marge had helped to mix large bowls of cookie dough for freezing — a basic recipe, to be divided later and made into eight varieties. But by now the cookies themselves should have been finished, ready for packing. And Gracie had meant to be well on her way with the salads and breads.

What's wrong with me, Lord, that I seem to take on more than I can possibly handle?

But then what could be omitted? She knew that Jesus would never turn his back on a child suffering a crisis of faith, nor on an adult whose basic insecurity poisoned her joy in the gift she had been given. And when He could casually feed five thousand, surely she should be able to handle — with minimal stress — eighty-plus senior citizens and assorted children.

And she hadn't even begun to delve into Sophie's problems yet.

I could never do it without You, Lord, any of it. I haven't the strength — physical, emotional or spiritual. I feel like such a pest, always asking You to help me through my minor crises — when there are millions of people clamoring for your attention at the same moment, all for much better reasons than mine!

I should be in the kitchen at this moment, mixing cheesecake, grating lemon peel, starting sauces — a thousand small, manageable steps toward what must be completed by tomorrow noon — and thanking You for the skills and the opportunity. Instead, I feel fragmented. And worried. And helpless.

She laid aside the cotton top she had planned to wear — since even in December, the temperature in the kitchen at baking time could seem tropical — and chose a dark green fleece walking suit. *But I am never helpless so long as I know You are with me.*

The best beginning to a catering day — or any day — was a brisk prayer-walk. *Thank*

You, Lord.

Gracie did preliminary bends and stretches while Charlotte Church sang Christmas carols in her ear. *Talk about glorious voices, Lord!*

Limbered up, she strode quickly past homes still huddled in semidarkness to the edge of town. *And it's not that I'm antisocial, Lord. There just isn't time for long conversations today — except with You.* For a time, she sang along with Charlotte, then muted the sound and did some serious planning. It was a crisp morning, the sun rising in tones of rose and gold against a clear sky. A great time for thinking. For planning. For praying, getting her priorities in line with His.

The catering event was to be held at Pleasant Haven Retirement Home. Residents had invited their families — many of whom lived at great distances — for an early Christmas celebration. Blaise Bloomfield, the social director, had designed activities for all ages, as well as inter-generational games and singing.

It was well-known to everyone but Pastor Paul himself that he had long been the object of her interest, but the down-to-earth Blaise was as patient as she was attractive. "Maybe by the time I'm fifty, do you think, he might notice me?" she'd asked Gracie once, with a rueful laugh. "For someone as bright as he is, he's really rather dense, isn't he?"

Dense enough, Gracie knew, to be fully oblivious to the admiration of countless young women in Willow Bend. The older ladies lavished him with attention, too. With their own sons grown and gone, the need remained to mother someone.

He received their gifts of baking and preserves with grace and charm, accepted their dinner invitations gratefully, always complimenting his hostess's culinary accomplishments to her complete satisfaction. When young women were also invited — with matchmaking in mind — he charmed them with his combination of boyish looks and pastoral sensitivity, then went home to his books and his current sermon, never noticing that he'd gently dented another heart.

"I've asked him to read portions of the Christmas story," Blaise had said with a wink when she met with Gracie to plan the afternoon's refreshments. "There'll be group singing — various carols. Would Amy do a solo, do you think? Maybe 'O, Holy Night'?"

Gracie paused to lean against the concrete

abutment of the bridge spanning Willow Creek. *Get me back on track, Lord, please. My mind's going in a dozen directions. Please calm my spirit, let me drink in the peace and beauty of this place, and return home ready to do what must be done. And let me do it with joy.*

She felt her pulse slow, her mind clear. She breathed in the pine-scented, crisp air. Sun highlighted the labyrinth of bare branches — maple, birch, poplar — that stood in stark silhouette against the sunrise. Oak leaves, clinging stubbornly, rattled in the breeze. The pine trees, however, huddled like a bevy of gossips in white lace shawls — while below and beyond the bridge, the creek gurgled beneath a thin sheath of ice.

How wonderful are Your works, Lord! Thank You for this place. This peace!

Gracie was nearing the end of her walk — starting to visualize the order of spices, icings and other ingredients that would make her work progress smoothly — when she heard singing. Only a thread, at first — but not an ordinary thread. More . . . like a tendril of spun silver enlivened by the stirring of the morning breeze. Thrilling!

But — she checked — yes, her tape was disengaged. It wasn't Charlotte Church.

For a moment, in the brisk stillness, her thoughts flashed to a sheep-dotted hillside outside Bethlehem, to shepherds, startled by an explosion of light and music that must have sounded much like this:

Gloria, gloria, gloria in excelsis deo —
Why do you lie slumbering
While prophecies unfold?
Can't You sense the stirring
Of the incense of the Ages?
Can't you see — beyond the clouds —
A glimpse of heaven's gold?

The glorious melody grew closer — just as the song of angels had once commanded that vast desert sky. Increasing in volume, it strengthened in timbre, its purity unabated.

Come, shake off your doubt and fright!
Shade your eyes from holy light;
From His vast celestial height
God approaches you tonight!
Gloria, gloria, gloria in excelsis deo!

Gracie — enthralled by the disembodied voice — found herself scarcely breathing. It seemed to come from nowhere — and from everywhere. Surely it bounced from rocks to achieve that echoing effect, or perhaps the chill of the air obscured its source.

Just as she was ready to believe that it might actually originate from heaven, she caught a glimpse of color rounding a deeply wooded bend in the narrow road. Brilliant color sparked with splinters of reflected light.

Maria?

She stifled the urge to call out.

Gloria, gloria, gloria in excelsis deo!
Why is it you hesitate,
Your knees unhinged by fear?
Still your trembling;
Give attention —
Could it be that you can doubt
The things you see and hear —

The lovely voice broke off as Willow Bend's newest soprano came into full view and recognized Gracie. Her face lit with pleasure and her arms flew wide. "Gracia! It is you, is it not? How so very fortunate to have meet you here, in this . . . forest!" Her graceful gesture embraced the wooded area. "I would like speech with you, yes?"

Gracie pushed aside her anxiety about all she must accomplish that day. There would be time enough. "We'll walk together!" she said, and added, "Yes?" Maria's speech patterns were obviously catching.

Despite her companion's age — perhaps a decade beyond Gracie's sixty-something — her pace easily matched Gracie's. Of course, Gracie thought, she's been on the stage, with all the discipline that entails. For a time, they spoke of the town, the cantata, the weather, the Christmas season.

After a comfortable silence, Gracie asked, "What is your favorite operatic role?"

Maria pursed her lips. "*Ah,* how I would so love to play the Carmen!"

"But you never have?"

Maria laughed. Even her laughter was musical, embracing at least two octaves. "Gracia, you mistake me! I have never play a major role, only perform in the chorus."

She sighed — a bit regretfully, Gracie thought.

"Such magnificent roles I was offer — a few, with small company. But there were my parents, you see." She patted Gracie's arm.

"Such parents," she said, "Mama so lovely and gifted. When she pluck the harp, such music she play, like from heaven itself. And then she lift from the oven wonderful cakes, always a celebration. And in her garden, everywhere the herbs and *such* roses!"

"And Papa —" she straightened her posture — "a man of true dignity. Until the soldiers come, and then broken. Haunted.

Such a sadness for Mama, for us all. And when her health falter as well —" She shrugged. "You can see how it had to be, Gracia, that I, the youngest and a daughter, must see to their care, once the others were married and gone. The opera must come second, even less, in my affections. I could be spared for the chorus, but never as prima donna."

She folded her hands over her heart. "And I would not have miss a moment I had with them, my wonderful mama and papa — not to be more famous than Callas!"

They walked in silence for a time, as snow began to fall in scattered flakes so large and pulpy that they splatted quietly on landing. Gracie thought gently of her own dear parents, and of El. For any of them — and of course for Arlen and his family in New York City — she too would happily have sacrificed fame, had it been offered.

"So beautiful!" Maria breathed. "This Willow Bend! You are so fortunate!" She paused. "Though we were fortunate, as well, in our small village — despite the harm we suffered."

She shuddered. "I was young barefoot girl when it all begin. When our beautiful safe world ends."

7

By the time Gracie reached home, the falling flakes had paused, leaving a half-inch or so of soft whiteness. The pattern of pawprints lacing her yard and Marge's proved that Gooseberry and Charlotte had been out for a game of chase.

Oops! Gracie went over to straighten the Christmas decoration in Marge's front yard — a now-antlerless deer, fashioned of small logs and twigs. One snapped leg lay beside it. Could Gooseberry and Charlotte actually be responsible?

The deer shouldn't be hard to mend, however. She'd ask Uncle Miltie —

Suddenly she saw her octogenarian uncle on a somewhat tipsy stepladder — his walker leaning against the porch rail. She gasped.

"Time to get some decorations up, if we don't want to look like Scrooges!" He called down to her as he juggled a tangle of lights.

"Can't make head nor tail of this." The ladder wobbled, and Gracie dashed anxiously to offer support. Mumbling an acknowledgment, he continued to fight the jumble of wire and bulbs. "Somebody must've had a lot of fun messing this up!" he grumbled, and Gracie decided not to mention who it was who had put them away the past January.

"Do come down, Uncle Miltie. Please. Right now. At least until you have it straightened. Then call, and I'll give you a hand." Giving the confusion of lights a vigorous shake, he descended.

"Breakfast's waiting for you," he grumbled. "Pancakes, bacon — you'll have to nuke them. I've already had mine." He banged the stubborn bundle against the porch rail — as though, Gracie thought, force would untie knots. "Gooseberry, too."

"Thanks." She gave him a quick kiss on his grizzled cheek. "You're a genius."

"A genius," he told her wryly, "would have done this already and had it up by now." She flashed a V for victory as she headed for the door. The last she glimpsed was a grimly determined expression on his face as he shook the tangled-up wires with renewed vigor.

Entering the warm house, she heard his

prediction that it was going to take him until next August to get the lights up and glowing. She was also pretty sure she heard a muttered "*Bah* humbug!"

The morning's baking, however, couldn't have gone more smoothly — so smoothly, in fact, that she totally forgot her uncle's dilemma until nearly lunchtime, when he entered snowy, red-cheeked and triumphant.

"You did it!" she exclaimed happily. "Congratulations!"

"Yes and no." He sank onto a chair, enjoying her puzzled look. "Take a peek, while I steal a cookie or two."

"Take all you like." She dusted her floury hands down her apron. "Up to six," she amended, as she stepped into the cold — a sweater thrown across her shoulders.

She nearly laughed aloud. The lights were hung — yes, but not completely untangled. In two places, Uncle Miltie had left the knots, with a resulting bundle of five or six bulbs bunched together. Still, the electricity managed to wriggle through, and she decided that at night the unique effect might even seem rather attractive.

"Well?" he asked when she re-entered. He waved a gumdrop cookie. "This is only number four, by the way."

"Well, it's certainly different," she replied. Affection as bright as the lights outside shone on her face. "It could even start a fad. Just imagine: the George Morgan style of holiday illumination!"

"Hmmph!" he said, with as much disdain as was possible with a mouth full of crumbs. But she could see he was secretly pleased.

Tish Ball and Tyne Anderson — long known to all of Mason County as the Turner twins, even though both were married — arrived for duty just after lunch. Marge appeared soon after. The twins donned identical checked gingham aprons over their designer blue jeans and white shirts embroidered with butterflies.

"Tell us what —" Tish began.

"— needs to be done," finished Tyne.

Marge carefully tied a transparent fuschia scarf over her upswept hair. "Just had it done." She patted it gently. "What do you think?" She turned for their inspection.

Tyne thought only for an instant before saying, "You look like —"

"— a model," Tish finished.

"Gracie?"

Gracie really wanted to say that she thought they should work now and praise hairdos later. But instead she smiled, saying, "Great, as always."

"Well," Marge said briskly, "why are we standing here yakking? Let's get to work!"

Since the cookies — set on stacked metal racks — were all but finished, already cooled, their icings drying, Gracie asked Marge to start the molded salads. "You always do such creative things with your layers!"

She then set the twins at the dining room table wrapping flatware in poinsettia-patterned napkins. She herself began to peel potatoes.

"Things seem to be coming along on schedule," Marge remarked, and Gracie agreed.

Thank You, Lord, she prayed, just as a knock rattled the front door.

"Oh, I can see you're busy!" Estelle Livett wore a fake fur jacket and a jaunty red knit cap. Her leather gloves were also red, as were her high-heeled shoes — clotted with snow.

Her feet must be frozen, Gracie thought, waving her in. Under her coat Estelle was wearing a brocade pants suit trimmed with antique lace. A large filigree brooch was pinned at the neck and another, even fancier one, rested over her heart.

"Never too busy for a friend," Gracie said brightly, though she hoped the "girls" would watch the potatoes. If there was anything she hated it was potato salad that looked as though it had been mashed through a sieve.

She took a moment to tell God that she knew why Estelle was so overdressed. *Because she feels insecure . . . and inadequate. Many women are like that, Lord.*

But then, He'd know that.

Gracie had done it herself, occasionally, when she felt particularly vulnerable — dressed in her best to give herself needed confidence. And while she hated to admit it, that had been the impetus behind having her hair colored the first time. "The brighter the better," she'd told the beautician. "I require more than a mere psychological boost: I need an explosion of confidence!"

When she'd first viewed the results, she'd had momentary cold feet. Within minutes, however, she'd determined that with the Lord behind her, sturdy shoes beneath her and this new flaming hair on top, she could face anything!

"You look lovely today, Estelle." Gracie indicated a comfy chair. "Please do sit down."

From the kitchen came a flurry of laughter

and the rattle-bang of kettles, Marge commanding, "Turn down the heat!"

Not the potatoes, Gracie hoped fervently. Please, not the potatoes.

Estelle hesitated. "I truly am afraid I'm interrupting. I don't want to be a bother. . . ." Her voice wobbled, and Gracie knew that of all places she wanted to be at this particular moment, she was right where she was most needed.

8

While Estelle composed herself, Gracie went to get tea and a plate of cookies.

Estelle waved the cookies away, took a sip of her tea and said firmly, "I'm dropping out of the choir."

Whatever Gracie might have expected, this was not it.

She set her cup and saucer down to still their rattling. "But, Estelle! Why ever would you want to do that?"

Before Estelle could answer with the obvious — or with a fiction designed to save face — Gracie continued. "What would we do without you? Your voice has been a mainstay for so long that losing it would be like . . . like . . . an amputation!"

Estelle shook her head. "Really, Gracie! I have never thought you given to hyperbole." But she was smiling, if only slightly.

Gracie pursued her advantage. "Haven't you noticed that as our choir has grown, so has our value? It's like adding ingredients to a fine stew. As each goes in, it seems initially to resist incorporation. But before you know it, everything is blended, and the stew has become richer for each addition."

Estelle wrinkled her nose. "I was never much for stew, myself. Although," she added quickly, "that chicken and dumpling mixture of yours at the last fellowship luncheon was quite tasty. What was your seasoning?"

"Basil. Celery, too — and of course onions."

"I went back for seconds. But really, Gracie, I can't think how this applies to choir! And I . . . I. . . ." She sighed. "I just feel that my particular skills are no longer appreciated." She preened a bit — suddenly back to the old Estelle Gracie knew so well, and often found so frustrating.

"I do have professional training, you know — from one of the best voice teachers in Chicago. He wanted me to go to Italy — to study opera —" She broke off, then repeated in a choked voice, "Italy . . . to . . . study —"

Gracie's heart squeezed. She yearned to reach out — physically — to this hurting woman. But she feared that Estelle would interpret a proffered hand as an expression of pity.

As perhaps it would be.

Lord, what can I say to this friend that will soothe her wounds, that will cause her to see and value her worth as Your child?

Self-worth had been the premise of Abe's story. That — and acceptance. But she could scarcely recite that wonderful fable for Estelle. She quieted her spirit, did reach to touch Estelle's arm — encountering no rejection — and began to speak softly.

"Remember when the Mackery baby died in her sleep — SIDS, I think it was — and the family and neighbors — all of Willow Bend, really — were so broken up? That tiny little angel in her pink and white casket not much bigger than a breadbox — it still makes me want to cry when I think of her. And at the cemetery — it was autumn, remember? You sang a lullabye — *a cappella* — and everyone was so moved."

Estelle's face had softened. "They sent me roses, later — as a thank you. And for years afterward, whenever I saw them —" Her voice tightened. "But that was then, Gracie — when I was appreciated! This is now."

"Then let me plead with you — now. Don't leave Barb — and the rest of us — in a bind with the cantata so far along. You're needed, Estelle! Give yourself at least until the new year to think it over. I have a feeling you'd miss us as much as we'd miss you!"

Estelle's mouth twisted. She pulled her arm from Gracie's touch, set her cup firmly on the end table and stood. "Gracie Lynn Parks, you may pull the wool over everyone else's eyes in this town — but you can't con me! Do you imagine for one minute I don't know what the other choir members think about me? Say about me? Do you think I don't see the glances in the congregation when I sing a solo? Not that it happens very often anymore! I will stay until after the cantata — not because you asked me, but because I'm a woman of my word. But after that —" She snapped her fingers. "— and then we'll see if young Amy and that show-offy Maria what's-her-name can carry the soprano section without me!"

Turning, she stalked from the room. As the door closed firmly behind her, Gracie hadn't moved. *Well, Lord, what do You make of that? Is it a good thing or a bad thing that she apparently has her confidence back?*

In the kitchen, Gracie met a battery of questions. She was still too stunned at Estelle's decision to say anything. Besides, she wanted to respect her friend's right not to be instantly everyone's topic number one.

"Gracie Lynn Parks, you're no fun!" scolded Marge, who, despite herself, found gossip as irresistible as Gracie deemed it potentially dangerous.

Tish offered, "I admire someone who —"

"— sticks to her principles!" Tyne finished loyally.

Uncle Miltie was always a great favorite at Pleasant Haven.

Actually, Uncle Miltie was a great favorite wherever he happened to be! Leave him off at the park and the children clustered about him like monarch butterflies around blooming milkweed. Take him to the grocery store, and women sought his manly opinion on how he preferred steak cooked; their husbands, it seemed, wouldn't say, just grumbled when it wasn't right.

Gracie was convinced that if he showed up at a quilting bee, the quilters would solicit his advice on their chosen pattern.

He waved at several acquaintances, then pointed to a group of flannel-shirted men. "I'll be over there if you need me," he said. "You have fun decorating." He waved and walked off, carrying his walker.

"He's looking quite spry today," Blaise said.

"He has good days . . . and bad days."

"Don't we all?" laughed Blaise.

Not at your age, Gracie thought. But she said, "Each one is a day the Lord has made, so I guess we shouldn't grumble." She rubbed the knuckles of her left hand. "On an afternoon like this — with all the wet snow — my arthritis kicks up. But that's a small price to pay for the beauty!"

Blaise glanced toward the window, the lower corners of each pane decorated with triangles of fluffy white. "It reminds me of when I was young — about twelve, I'd guess. We had a snow like this, and I was absolutely enamored — picturing each fluffy flake as a ballerina — or an angel.

" 'Isn't it beautiful?' I asked my grandmother — the grumpy one. And she said, 'Beautiful enough, I guess, until it gets inside your boots.' " She sighed. "I never understood how anyone could hate snow."

She gave a gesture of dismissal. "Maybe she had arthritis, too. Would you rather help trim a tree or hang garlands from the rafters?"

When the large room was fully decorated, Gracie was sure all the children would love it. Ceramic gingerbread men, wooden nut-crackers, strings of functional sleighbells, large iridescent snowflakes, angels and three-dimensional stars appeared every-where. Plush poinsettias and red velvet rib-bons caught fat garlands in generous loops. And, most impressive of all, a lovely Nativ-ity made of olive wood stood on a pedestal in the center of the room.

"Amy will stand next to it, I think. She did say she'd sing? I hope so!"

Gracie gave a start. "Was I supposed to ask her?" she asked with a guilty look.

Blaise hastened to assure her, "No, no, I was only worrying. It's the one thing I've neglected. All the catering — and now decorating . . . Gracie, you'd better take Uncle Miltie home and get some rest. I'm certain there are last-minute things you'll need to do in the morning."

"You're right. And, of course, Amy will come and sing . . . gloriously."

Blaise paused to take an admiring look around the room. "All this — it's so beauti-ful, isn't it? Christmas decorations always cheer me up! But, you know, I'm not sure we can really ask her on such short no-tice. . . ."

Gracie nodded. "Might have to work —"

She broke off. "But you have Maria right here!"

"Maria? Buonarotti?" Impulsively, Blaise hugged her. "That's inspired! I should have thought —" She shrugged. "I guess I just wasn't sure if she'd be here for the holidays, especially since she's leaving so soon after!"

"Maria's . . . leaving? She just got here!"

Blaise took a moment to adjust a garland. "You didn't know we were just a temporary solution for her? She's planning to live with her sister in Chicago, but she's having her apartment redone." She paused. "But, meanwhile, Maria's ours! It just proves, doesn't it — once again — that all things work together for good?"

"When we allow them to," Gracie agreed.

Now — why did this exchange make her think of Estelle, Patsy and Sophie, too? *Please, Lord, may all things work together for their joy this Christmas season.*

When Uncle Miltie rejoined her, Gracie had reason to expand her prayer to cover all of Willow Bend.

"It's become an epidemic!" he said. "This Christmas decoration thing. Or maybe I should say desecration?"

"Oh?"

"The guys were saying." He frowned. "It's amazing how the grapevine beats out the

74

newspaper every time!"

"What *about* the decorations?"

"Rocky's said it often enough — who needs reporters, when you can hear the news anywhere a few people get together?"

"The decorations —" she prompted.

"They're missing. All over town. Mrs. Cooper's Grinch was nearly new. First a tree branch falls on it, breaking off one arm and then — *poof!* It's gone." He shook his head. "I could have patched it for her in ten minutes. In fact, I was going to offer."

"And there are others? Besides a candy cane and an elf. I heard about those."

"Part of a Nativity set — one of those light-up plastic ones? A snowball broke a Wise Man's crown. Gone. Even the broken piece. And a sleigh at Watsons' — one of the runners. Why, Gracie, even that dumb little deer of Marge's —"

"Gone?"

"Poof!" He spread his arms wide. "Doesn't the Bible warn about this — in the End Times?"

"Earthquakes. Rumors of wars. All kinds of frightening and horrible diasters — but, frankly, I have to say that I don't remember missing reindeer being mentioned!"

He chuckled, then sobered. "Gracie, who around here would do something like this?"

75

She had no idea. But she knew Who would know.

Silently, she added a codicil to her prayer.

9

As luck would have it, Sophie was by the cash register at the Deli when Gracie took Uncle Miltie out to try the new Saturday breakfast buffet. Not luck, Gracie amended her thoughts. Providence. *Thank You, Lord!*

Uncle Miltie paused in the complicated process of removing his wraps. Gracie wanted to help — and would have, at home — but suspected it might wound his pride in public.

Sophie, however, bustled over, eased his walker from his grasp and said soothingly, "Now, you just take your time at the buffet. Old bones don't react well to damp and cold, do they? We should *all* be in Florida right now!" she clucked.

"You can't convince Abe, and you can't convince me. God made snow for a reason."

"Well, He made palm trees, too!" Sophie retorted.

"Speaking of bones," Uncle Miltie said,

changing gears. "What did one bone say to another?" His eyes twinkled.

Sophie pursed her lips and rolled her eyes upward. "No idea," she said at last.

Uncle Miltie rubbed his hands in anticipation. "Let's get together at some hip joint."

Neither Gracie nor Sophie could refrain from giggling. Still smiling, Sophie turned to head for the kitchen.

Uncle Miltie selected a variety of miniature muffins. "A lady of rare good taste, that Sophie!" He lined them up on his plate: cranberry, orange, lemon, blueberry.

Sophie called, "I'm surprised to see you here, Gracie! Isn't the Pleasant Haven luncheon today?"

"Everything's ready!" Gracie said.

"My goodness! I always feel like a pup chasing his tail! I've decided I'll never catch up."

Gracie laughed. "There's that Pennsylvania Dutch saying —"

"Something like 'the hurrieder I go the behinder I get?' " Uncle Miltie supplied. "Well, cut the chitchat! Let's eat!"

Her uncle had heaped his plate with enough saturated fats to fell an elephant. A judgmental attitude, she admitted to herself, would seem hypocritical, considering the rich ingredients she used in her own cooking. He was looking down at his food appreciatively.

"I'm pretty well set up here." He grinned. "But I could use a bit more butter — the real stuff — and more syrup, if you don't mind."

"And grapefruit?" she suggested, noticing there was no fruit on his tray, unless you counted the bits in the little muffins.

He shrugged. "Later, maybe, if I still have room."

Uncle Miltie was back for seconds — still no grapefruit, Gracie observed — when Abe emerged from the kitchen.

"Best place in the world to keep cozy and warm on a day like this." He pulled out a chair for himself.

"Cozy is not how I'd describe the command center of Willow Bend's most popular restaurant. But I'm sure the kitchen is warm!"

Sophie appeared with a platter of refills for the buffet table. "I hope you two are enjoying the buffet! Would you like some of these slices of French toast?"

Uncle Miltie brightened. "I'll drink a toast to that," he said, raising his coffee mug.

Sophie turned, spatula in hand. "Or could I give you some quiche, dear —"

Gracie held out her plate. "I guess I need

some extra energy for later on. Thanks."

"If you can't beat 'em, join 'em," Uncle Miltie winked.

"I feel like I'm in training for the breakfast-buffet Olympics! How much can I turn out how fast? But it's fun, really!" Sophie winked back at Uncle Miltie.

"If that woman's depressed," Uncle Miltie declared as they made their way slowly to Fannie Mae's parking spot, "then I'm a ringtailed hoot owl."

Gracie opened the door of her venerable blue Cadillac and supported her uncle's elbow as he inched into the passenger seat. Only when he was in and his seatbelt fastened did she say, "She certainly seemed fine today. Though when you were going back for *fourths* —" she paused for emphasis — "Abe mentioned to me that a phone call late last night had brightened her considerably."

"From Florida?"

"Maybe someone reporting that her dogs are doing well."

"*Hmmph!* Should have brought them with her."

"But they're not used to cold weather. And she didn't want to uproot them . . . disrupt their routines."

80

"A child, she'd bring along."

Gracie had thought the same herself. She herself couldn't bear to leave Gooseberry for weeks on end.

"You know what I think?" Uncle Miltie asked quietly. "I think our Sophie has a beau."

Gracie nearly steered Fannie Mae into a snow-covered hedge. "My goodness, let me think about that," she replied.

"Mark my words," was all Uncle Miltie would say. "And make sure you get us home safely."

10

There was little, Gracie thought, that could match the pleasure of an event coming off perfectly. At Pleasant Haven, the tables, draped with spotless white linen, held ornate brass candleholders. Blaise said, "We've pulled the drapes, so even though it's a bright day outside, the candlelight will have its proper effect."

In one corner, Santa's sleigh stood heaped with wrapped and beribboned gifts. Naturally, the few children arriving early headed straight for it. Gracie heard them exclaiming over the display and admired their restraint.

An overhead spotlight centered on the Nativity, which had been set up to turn slowly on its pedestal. Piped-in Christmas carols helped create the illusion that the display was, in reality, a giant music box. Gracie stood for a moment, appreciating the figures — carved with simple elegance and polished to a golden sheen.

Blaise appeared beside her. "Beautiful, isn't it?"

"Glorious. From the Holy Land?"

"A village near Jerusalem. Mrs. Melwood donated it. There she is, just entering the room."

Gracie saw a distinguished-looking blue-haired lady walking with slow dignity, her progress aided by a silver-headed cane.

"Ebony?" guessed Gracie.

"Or mahogany. She's a new resident. Fascinating! She and her husband circled the globe — many times. She's ninety-four! Can you imagine still traveling abroad in your nineties?"

It sounded wonderful to Gracie.

Without pausing, Blaise continued her thumbnail sketch of the new resident.

"When Mr. Melwood suffered a fatal heart attack — chopping wood, if you can believe it! — only months after the Nativity set arrived in crates, his wife found their Chicago mansion echoing with loneliness. As she puts it, 'Of what use are luxurious possessions if there is no one with whom to share their beauty?' "

With obvious appreciation and respect, Blaise continued her narrative. It appeared that Mrs. Melwood had retained only a few loved pieces from the years of extensive travels with her husband. The Nativity was one of them.

"She said that only one of her children has room enough for such a large display — but that he didn't want it. So she gave it to us!" Blaise fairly glowed. "What an unbelievable gift — and all Mrs. Melwood wants in recompense is to enjoy it each Christmas. With her new friends here."

Moments later, the lady herself paused by the circling manger scene. She reached out to touch it gently — but, in fact, her fingertips never quite made contact with the gleaming wood. She smiled softly, seeming oblivious to all that surrounded her — except for the Nativity.

Lord, she's remembering, isn't she — reliving the day they discovered it together? Gracie's own eyes filled with tears. *She's feeling as I do when I come across something El and I bought together, having fallen in love with it.*

She found herself dabbing at her eyes. *Oh, Lord, only You truly know how much I miss that dear man!*

"Earth to Gracie," Blaise was saying, laughter in her voice. "Your crew is waiting for their captain!"

They certainly were.

Marge, Barb Jennings and the Turner twins were aproned and eager.

"I was just . . . reminiscing," Gracie said.

Blaise sighed. "Memory is at once one of God's greatest gifts and —" She didn't finish the thought.

She didn't need to. Gracie knew. Remembering could cause a splinter in the heart, a sudden cramping of the spirit, an ache that consumed mind, body and soul in a blending of regret and gratitude.

And yet, Gracie told God as she went to help her friends arrange the tables, *for all the pain, I wouldn't want to lose a single memory!*

Were compliments legal tender, Gracie and her crew could have counted themselves rich even before the main course was being enjoyed by the contented crowd.

"Your croutons — the best I've ever tasted!"

"Do you mix your own salad dressings?"

"And the bread! Who else would have thought of onion flakes and parsley?"

"Even the butter —"

"And the salad greens!"

And on and on and on.

Tish gushed, "Your catering's always a hit, Gracie, but —"

"— this is extreme!" Tyne contributed.

Marge explained, "The difference is who's eating it. Some of these people have been everywhere, sampling the cuisine of many cultures." She shrugged. "They recognize cooking from the heart when they taste it!"

Barb nodded. "Once they get to the stuffed chicken breast, they'll be ready to carry you out of here on their shoulders."

Gracie reminded her helpers, "Hey, we're all in this together, aren't we? Where would I be without all of you?"

Tish pondered, "Maybe chef —"

"— on a cruise ship! They have the best food —"

"At least that's what we've heard."

A deeper voice said, "Sounds like my favorite cook is reaping some well-deserved praise."

Gracie smiled gently. "Rocky thinks he's capable of judging whether a meal's any good or not. But, really, it's quantity he goes for — the more mashed potatoes, the happier he is. A lone pork chop makes him nervous. . . ."

"Hey, that's not fair! I'm simply an honest eater, and, honestly, Gracie, I think you're a magnificent chef!"

Gracie blushed.

Rocky's salt-and-pepper hair glinted in

the muted light. In honor of the occasion, he had dressed a bit more formally than usual, though his jacket pocket bulged with notebook and pen, and a black satchel hung heavy over his shoulder.

Gracie regarded him. "You've come to get a story, of course."

He mock-saluted.

She laughed. He *was* one of her favorite people. "Come on, let's cut the dessert."

Obeying, the twins spoke over their shoulders:

"We're looking forward to —"

"— Maria, when she sings."

Rocky caught Gracie's arm. "*The* Maria?" he asked, "the one who's ruffled Estelle's peacock feathers?"

"The same. Oh, there she comes now."

If Maria's outfits before had been flamboyant, today she was beyond theatrical. Way beyond. Cleopatra — even as played by Elizabeth Taylor — would have paled in contrast. She seemed aflame with sequins, glass beads, bangles and medallions.

Rocky murmured, "A bit overdressed, are we?"

"She's a professional opera singer, remember. Or was."

"And that explains why she's wearing a fireworks display?"

Gracie wisely decided that anyone with chemically enhanced fire-engine-red hair should probably withhold comment.

Besides, Lord, Maria's expressing herself. So she's a bird of paradise among wrens and swallows! When she begins to sing, who can possibly care?

"O, holy night. . . ." The first pure, vibrant notes brought a sudden deep hush to the candlelit room. It was as though all breathing was suspended. No chairs creaked, no child whimpered, no foot shuffled. Gracie fancied that in the pauses between glorious phrases she could even hear the candle flames sputtering.

And when the final note throbbed to a sustained whisper, there was a deep, living silence. Moments later the room echoed with applause. Chairs scraped, then the audience was on its feet. Maria bowed extravagantly, her face beaming beneath her masses of piled dark hair and sparkling tiara.

When finally Santa interrupted with his *"Ho, ho, ho!"* Maria's glance found Gracie. "Oh, Gracia, my perfect friend!" she gushed. Moving with a swooshing rustle of skirts and the blinding twinkle of ornaments, she swept Gracie into her glittery embrace. "So sweet you are to have listen —"

Suddenly, her face blanched. She staggered, finding support in a serving cart.

"Maria!" Her voice shrill with alarm, Gracie reached to steady her. Oh, dear me, is she having an attack of some sort? Was the stress too great? Her own heart raced.

"Here, Maria. Please let me help you to a chair —"

But Maria seemed not to hear. Her wide eyes were fastened beyond, on —

Rocky?

Releasing the cart carefully, Maria moved unsteadily toward him — he backing slightly away — and her voice throbbed with emotion. "I had think never to see you again, Rocco my love, my hero, the liberator of my village! For long years I have grieve that you were disappeared, lost to me." Her voice broke. "But here — where I have come for such short time — I find you, and I thank the good God above that you are restore to me!"

11

"You remind her of someone else, that's all."

They were in Gracie's kitchen, sipping tea. Rocky's face was a study in recovery from terror.

"I didn't know what to say!" He groaned for perhaps the twentieth time.

"You couldn't have spoken anyway, with your mouth hanging open like that." Gracie offered him a plate of cinnamon toast squares. "Here's something to help calm you down."

Uncle Miltie, stroking Gooseberry, reflected, "That's sure one intimidating . . . lady. About my age, would you say?"

Marge proposed, "Just right, *huh,* Uncle Miltie? I'm a veteran matchmaker."

"George Morgan to you," he growled, and she sat back, satisfied at having provoked him. "Matchmaker!" he snorted under his breath.

Gracie shook her head. Why couldn't her

best friend and her dear uncle declare a temporary truce at least?

Deciding that the best course of action was to try to answer her uncle's question, she said, "She's only in her seventies, I think."

"But you look so young for your age, Unc — Mr. Morgan."

"Hmmph!" he grunted.

Rocky took a gulp of tea. "I know you're right, Gracie — mistaken identity. But how can we convince her of that? Until we do, I'm going to feel like a mouse with an eagle stalking me."

Marge raised an eyebrow. "Man or mouse?" she teased.

Uncle Miltie snapped, "This is serious stuff, here! Rocky's no mouse but he's right to sense a trap closing around him. . . ." He turned to Rocky. "You were just a kid back then. Maybe if we tell her that —"

"We tried," moaned Rocky. "We tried."

Marge said, "She didn't seem to think you were lying —"

"— as much as you were confused," Gracie said.

"Or trying to avoid her." Rocky swept a hand through his hair and shut his eyes for a second. "Ashamed of abandoning her all those years ago." He said in desperation,

"How could a teenager hang on to a crush like that, anyway? After so many decades. . . ."

"It was wartime." Uncle Miltie reminded him. He continued, "Everything's more . . . intense, then. On edge. Danger makes everything sharper."

"It's pretty sad." Marge reached for a piece of toast. "But fascinating, too. Romantic!"

"I guess the question is . . . what do we do now?" Gracie poured herself another mug of tea.

"I don't want to hurt her feelings," Rocky said. "That's for sure."

"But right is right!" Uncle Miltie insisted. "You also don't want to have to skulk through the shadows in order to avoid the amorous advances of an elderly opera singer! Mistaken identity or not, she seems pretty determined!"

"Think, Rocky!" Marge now urged him. "Not that you haven't been! But I've read everyone has at least one double —"

"With the same name?" Uncle Miltie scoffed. He frowned. "Which brings up a good question. How could she recognize him after all these years? Really, it seems obvious that she's remembering someone who years and years ago resembled the

Rocky of today!"

Gracie looked at her uncle with respect. "You're right — while Maria's infatuation might not have changed, the object of it certainly would have! So we need to consider a man who, fifty or sixty years ago, looked something like Rocky now!"

They all stared at him accusingly.

Gracie pointed out, "Hey, we're all pretty tired and we need fresh minds if we're to work this out before Rocky enters a witness protection program of some kind." She reached for Rocky's hand. "When did your family come to America?"

Gooseberry yawned. Human dramas bored him and usually wound up robbing him of the attention he believed was his due.

Rocky answered, "My father's family left Italy in 1910. Dad was the youngest. There were three sisters and three — no, four — brothers."

Uncle Miltie asked sharply, "The uncle you nearly forgot to count?"

"The oldest. I don't remember ever seeing him. Mom said he had itchy feet —" he grinned — "and for a long time, when I was little, I wondered why he didn't simply get some foot powder and stop the itching. Dad called it wanderlust, and only shook his head — whether in sadness or envy, I was never quite certain. Once every so often, when we were young, Dad would get a postcard from somewhere — South Africa, where my uncle worked for a short time in a diamond mine. In Tibet I think he was studying to be a monk, next. But that didn't last long, either."

"Did your dad ever get a card from Italy?" Gracie asked quietly.

He nodded. "That was home, after all —" He stiffened. "What are you thinking, Gracie?"

With suppressed excitement she asked, "So what was this roving uncle's name?"

Rocky clapped his hand to his head. "Of course! I was named for him! Dad insisted I was Uncle Rocco's 'spittin' image!' "

"What a relief!" Marge exclaimed. "We figured it out!"

"Whew!" said Rocky.

"Double *whew!*" echoed Uncle Miltie.

"Well, that's only one mystery down." They all cheered. "But what about the plague of missing decorations?" Gracie asked, certain that Rocky would be relieved to consider a puzzle that didn't involve him — at least not in a personal way.

He told them, grinning, "None other than Mayor Thomas Ritter himself honored the *Gazette* with his presence today!"

"Oh, brother!" Marge said.

"Did you videotape it for posterity?" Uncle Miltie teased.

Rocky ignored him. "His Honor, you won't be surprised to hear, is quite incensed by 'Willow Bend's current crime wave.' He reminded me of my civic duty."

"Hmmph!" was all Uncle Miltie could say. And Gracie agreed.

"He wrote a story himself." Rocky's eyes now twinkled. "It took Jess most of the afternoon to make it publishable."

"What was it?" Uncle Miltie scoffed. "First chapter of his autobiography?"

"Just about. Ten pages reduced to five column inches, once Jess deleted the political posturing and self-aggrandizement, not to mention the sentimental wallowing in the true spirit of Christmas and the rights of all Americans to decorate their houses with elves and snowmen unmolested by evil-doers."

In the shared laughter that followed, Gracie felt a sense of — was it guilt? It had always been one of her family maxims that no matter how crusty the outside, everyone had a soft center. The problem was, while the Ritters weren't exactly crusty, they most certainly were brittle.

"Deep down," she insisted, "the Ritters

have good in them." But her expression wasn't entirely convincing.

"Deep down," Uncle Miltie contributed dryly, "a wormy apple has a core. But we still don't swallow the apple."

Estelle wasn't in church Sunday morning. Neither was Maria — but Gracie felt sure the latter, at least, would be at the afternoon practice.

"I can't believe how time is getting away from us!" Barb groaned. "From now on, it's at least two practices a week!"

For the anthem, they sang one of the songs from the cantata. It was a gentle piece — to Gracie reminiscent of Christina Rossetti's lovely lyrics.

I am a lamb — tiny and cuddly soft,
And *baaing* gently as the baby sleeps.
I tremble slightly in the brilliant light
And watch how gentle Mary keeps
Her fingertips close to the baby's form . . .
And how she huddles close
To keep Him warm.
    When I am grown — a sheep,
Covered with curling fleece . . .
    When He is grown — a man, and brave
    and strong —
I wonder if my wool might make a robe

For Him to wear when nights are cold and
   long.
   By then, the size of starlight
Might have dimmed,
And there might be . . .
   No angel song.

The hush that followed as Barb struck the
final trembling chord was so complete that
Gracie could hear the ticking of Pastor
Paul's small clock on the lectern and the
hum of warm, circulating air.

And then a communal murmur accompanied the rustling of bulletins.

" 'I am a lamb,' " Pastor Paul repeated.
"What a cozy image! A lamb — no burrs,
no fleas, of course — caught into the Master's arms and cuddled there. What a safe
place to be! What a safe place to rest, to
escape the cares of the world and the
consequences of our actions! We all yearn
to be such a lamb, don't we?"

He set his notes aside, leaned on the
lectern and spoke from his heart. "This was
not my sermon for the day. No, I planned
to follow tradition and present that sweet,
sanitized stable we so comfortably portray
at Christmas time. No unpleasant odors of
animal waste or fouled hay or human sweat.
No splinters, no pain of childbirth, no ques-

tions or fears. Just that sweet scene we cherish because it demands nothing of anyone.

"The trouble is, dear friends, that lambs become sheep — willful, distracted, straying — just like us. The baby Jesus grew up as one of us — and that meant tears and frustration, pebbles caught in worn-through sandals, scorching heat by day and chill by night — and, to the shame of humanity, the torture and death of the cross.

"But we aren't supposed to think of wrenching pain and torn flesh at this season, are we? Save it for Eastertide — and, with any luck, we can skip the betrayal of Thursday, the agonies of Friday, the despair of Saturday, and go straight from Palm Sunday to Easter."

He paused, and some congregants shifted uneasily.

Lord, they're concerned about their children, hearing this. They're decorating, wrapping gifts, celebrating with friends and family. They — rather, we — don't want to think about the cross, not now.

While Pastor Paul's voice continued — earnest, pleading — Gracie spent her time in private prayer. And when her attention turned again to what he was saying, she could tell he was winding down.

"Our Savior began his life in a rude

wooden structure — and ended it nailed to another. And if that had been the end of it, a body hanging limp and bloody on a cross, how sad. Rather than dwelling on his terrible death, however, let us recall this Christmas why He went to the cross. Not because the Romans willed it, but because it was God's gift to the world — all the people who have lived, or ever will. God gave us a very special gift in the swaddled baby form of His Son. Both of them reinforced that gift of love on Calvary."

"It has to be a quick lunch — at least for me." Gracie settled into the chair Rocky held for her.

Rocky grinned at Abe. "That means none of your marathon stories!"

Abe shook his head. "You really know how to hurt a guy." He handed them menus. "The special's stuffed cabbage, Sophie's own recipe. She made it before she left." His face shadowed.

"Left?" Gracie repeated. "She went back to Florida?"

"No. Just home. She . . . wasn't feeling well. I'll get your drinks. The usuals?"

While Rocky studied the menu, Gracie sent up a prayer.

I should drop by to see Sophie — but how

can I? Barb needs everyone at practice, and it's liable to go until dinnertime.

"Maybe I'll drop by your house this evening," she said, as Abe set their ice water and steaming coffee before them. "If you think she wouldn't mind."

"There's no one she'd rather see." He dropped his hand to her shoulder. "Thanks, my friend."

Estelle was late to cantata practice, and her expression was strained as she sat — not in the choir loft at all, but in the third pew.

Barb turned, her baton on hold. "Come on, Estelle!" Her tone dropped in concern. "You're not ill, are you? That flu that's already hit Mason City?"

Estelle answered cryptically. "Not ill. Not flu."

"Well, then!" Apparently unaware that Estelle hadn't moved, Barb resumed tapping out the time.

If angels should appear
In any nighttime sky of mine,
I wonder if they'd find me
    tending sheep —
Or find me caught in aimless
    wandering —
    Or fast asleep.

Barb clapped her hands sharply. "No, no, no! Not right! We need more high soprano there! Estelle — *Estelle!* Where are you?"

The third pew was empty.

For a moment, Gracie feared that Estelle was gone — but she had only moved farther back in the sanctuary.

Barb propped both fists on her hips. The baton twitched. "Estelle, are you coming or not?"

Estelle gave a tense glance at the soprano section. "Are you certain — absolutely certain — that you need me?"

"Of course we need you!" snapped Barb. "We need everyone!"

Les Twomley grumbled, "What does she want? An engraved invitation?" and Marge whispered, "I thought only opera singers stormed off in pique!"

But Maria, Gracie noticed, seemed quite content to be surrounded by lesser talents.

How often, Lord, we find the true humility in those who have the most reason to be over-bearing!

Estelle sat, apparently considering.

"Coming or not?" Barb snapped.

Estelle, pausing a few minutes more, finally stood and moved into the aisle, heading for her usual place with the group.

But she changed direction when she heard

Maria urge softly, "Please, Estella, *cara,* give us your most lovely music."

Estelle stiffened, turned, and marched to the rear of the sanctuary.

"As you wish," Barb said tightly to the door, watching it shut behind Estelle. "Hit it, folks!"

Waken me, Lord, with vivid light
From some bright guiding star. . . .

Poor Estelle, Gracie thought. *Poor hurting Estelle. What are we going to do for her, Lord?*

12

Gracie had hoped to escape before Maria demanded to know more about Rocky. But Barb wanted to discuss light refreshments for those attending the cantata; Don Delano needed to know how to make caramel corn balls as a special Christmas treat for the high school science club; Amy waited to confide increasing concern for Patsy Clayton — and, thus, Maria, patient and smiling, joined the queue before Gracie could forestall her.

I really need to see Estelle, Lord. And I promised Abe to stop by to talk with Sophie. Oh, and how could I have forgotten dear little Patsy, in the rush of everything else? And what can I possibly say to Maria? Help!

For choir practice, Maria had toned down her wardrobe — somewhat. While her billowing smock was patterned with brilliant hibiscus, there were no sequins, rhinestones or beads, and her long skirt was plain black, save for a border echoing the flaming pink, orange and red of the hibiscus.

"Dear Gracia, I have wait to speak with you." Maria smiled shyly, expectantly.

Gracie suddenly realized how weary she had become. "Could we sit?"

"But of course. You have the time?"

Gracie nodded — an outright lie, she thought guiltily, even if unspoken.

"Good!" Maria gathered her skirts and plunked down on the pew beside Gracie. "It is about Rocco, I would speak. Yes?" Without waiting for an answer she said, "All night I toss and turn, thinking. Remembering. It was as though I climbed the hot sandy piles of tumbled stones again, that once were the proud buildings of my village. As though I skinned my knees on roughness, and searched for tiny lizards I might keep for a while for my very own. And there was Rocco — not in a uniform but —"

Her eyelids, half-closed, failed to hide the stars. "To him, I was a scrawny little girl — that I now know. To me he was a —" she drew a quivering breath — "my . . . idol. Yes! I knew that to be evil, that old Father Antonio would give me a thousand 'Hail Marys' for penance, and that my grandmother — though scarcely as tall as I —

104

would punish me in ways even more terrible. But, Gracia — perhaps you understand, if you have been in love, there was no help for me. I was powerless. I worshiped him."

In the silence, Gracie wondered if there were something she should say, but before it could come to her, Maria continued. "It was hoped, when American soldiers came, there would be chocolate bars for the children. But Rocco Gravino was not American — he was Italian, and as poor as we. However, the day he found me crying, my knee bleeding, and my spirit shredding from terror — he brought me a flower! It was beautiful, and the first flower anyone had give me, ever — and he was also beautiful, this first man who made my heart beat! He was old enough, yes, to be my papa, but that make no difference. Do you understand, dear Gracia?"

Gracie nodded. It was impossible to speak, with a throat so full.

Maria leaned forward. "I know from what you say, what I did not hope to hear, that this Rocco Gravino is not my Rocco Gravino. How old he would be, by now — for I, too, am old. But this man — who is not the one I love — is so like him, that I wonder if it would much grieve him if I adore him. Just a little." She measured with her thumb and forefinger. "And I will do it silently, perhaps when he is not watching, only that the Rocco I knew as a child will live again for brief moments in my heart."

Gracie was still incapable of speech. She looked at Maria with brimming eyes and they hugged tightly. Rocky, Gracie knew, would not mind at all.

Estelle was quite another matter — or, as Uncle Miltie might have put it, "a horse of a different color." As Gracie approached the porch, she saw a curtain twitching. Pretending not to notice, she made a bit more noise than necessary as she mounted the steps, carefully swept her boots free of snow, and rang the bell. Deliberately, she hummed a tune from the cantata.

No answer.

She pushed the doorbell again, then rapped on the door.

No answer.

This particular number had an obligato suited to voices such as Estelle's or Maria's — even Amy's — but certainly not to Gracie's alto range. Praying that she wouldn't irreparably strain her vocal chords, she pitched her voice as high as it would go and screeched the overtune.

It was terrible! Inwardly, she smiled, continuing. A neighbor's dog howled. *Ouch!*

Within Estelle's foyer, she now heard a scrambling and a fumbled latch.

"Gracie Lynn Parks," Estelle demanded, throwing the door open, "do you have any idea how you sound?"

Gracie did, but had no time to answer as Estelle tugged her inside and slammed the door behind them. "God knew what he was doing when he made you an alto! Whatever's gotten into you?"

Gracie said innocently, "I thought I should try, just to see how it sounded —"

"Please promise me not to try again!" Estelle interrupted her.

Gracie pretended not to notice. "— Just in case," she continued. "Barb's going to have to use whatever voices she has available."

"Barb would never — she has too much sense! I may not always agree with her choice of music, or the way she parcels out solos, but she's too good a director to give an alto a high soprano part!"

"I suspect you're right," Gracie said meekly.

Waving Gracie into an easy chair and taking the matching couch herself, Estelle fell suddenly silent.

I overplayed it, didn't I, Lord? Gracie asked. *Now she's suspicious.* She looked around the semi-dark living room. Estelle was given to the rich hues found in peacock feathers, and Gracie had to admit that the combination of turquoise, midnight blue, various purples and greens was beautiful — in a funereal kind of way. Gracie herself preferred rooms filled with light and air.

Yet without a doubt Estelle had chosen her fabrics well, and the antique-framed floral prints on the emerald green wall unified the decor. "I like what you've done here, Estelle," she said — and her admiration was every bit as sincere as her singing performance had been counterfeit.

Estelle had begun drumming her fingertips on the marble top of a small end table.

Gracie fought the desire to turn her way, to read her expression.

Finally, Estelle cleared her throat. "This charade was totally unnecessary," she said tonelessly. "You've wasted my time and yours — and very likely ruined your own voice — at least for the cantata. Perhaps forever."

Gracie stirred.

"And don't pretend you don't understand," Estelle warned. "Really, Gracie, your manipulations are so transparent! Besides, I promised that I'd see the cantata through — and I will. It was just that — that woman infuriated me." Estelle stood, emphasizing the personal pronouns in her next statements.

"*I'm* the one who's gone to Eternal Hope since I was baptized. The choir members are *my* friends, not hers — and more family than friends, much of the time. She's just here temporarily at Pleasant Haven! Let her go sing at Waxmire or Trinity. . . ."

She stiffened, pointing an index finger in Gracie's direction. "And then . . . then . . . she presumed — in front of *my* friends, in *my* church — to . . . to order me about!"

She was nearly sputtering, giving Gracie no opening to demur.

But what can I say, Lord, that won't make things even worse? I can't urge her to give Maria a chance, to recognize the woman's basic goodness, to accept her amazing talent as a gift, not a threat. She has to come to that point by herself. And Estelle herself is a good person, she really is.

Gracie wondered whom she was trying to convince — herself or God?

But that wasn't fair to either of them.

She and Estelle were friends. But it was not with the old-shoe style of friendship Gracie and Marge enjoyed, and not with the challenging banter that so often ensued when she, Abe and Rocky were together. It wasn't like the easy relationship Gracie had when she and her catering crew worked together, either. With Estelle, any relationship would necessarily be prickly.

Estelle had grown quiet. "I won't offer refreshments, Gracie. That might indicate hospitality, and I don't want to be hypocritical." Her composure rumpled. "On top of my other shortcomings."

"Estelle —"

Estelle shook her head. "No, Gracie, don't try to placate me. You've done quite enough damage here for one day. Why don't you just go home?"

13

"I can't talk about it. At least not yet." Holding an ice pack to her forehead, Sophie managed a slight smile perhaps to compensate for what might seem brusqueness. "I do appreciate your coming, more than I can say." She sighed. "I wish . . . Abe. . . ." She sighed again.

"You couldn't ever disappoint Abe," Gracie said softly.

Sophie started. "How — did you know —"

"Actually, I don't *know* anything. But what else could give you such pain?"

Sophie laid aside the ice pack. "You're right, of course. But I'm still not quite ready. . . ."

"Why don't I make us some tea, and we'll talk about any subject in the world. Except that one."

Sophie laughed. "You're the best thing since penicillin, Gracie Lynn Parks! Let me make the tea!"

Gracie sat peacefully thinking, as she waited for Sophie to return. Gazing around her, she noticed the absence of personalizing touches.

Of course Sophie's true home remained in Florida. There she would have the family keepsakes, the furniture worn to the shape of her body, the purchases made on impulse. Gracie often thought that what she herself bought on impulse held important clues to her character, her interests, even her small addictions.

Why else would she have duplicates of every spice known to humanity — even though a few bought years ago still had unbroken seals? Why else did she have three subscriptions for *Guideposts* magazine? She didn't really need one each for her bedroom, the living room and the upstairs bathroom!

Or, perhaps she did. That way, inspiration was close at hand, whenever she had a few spare moments to learn of the faith of others, the miracles that had touched their lives.

Gracie was a bit startled to see an open copy of *Daily Guideposts* on Sophie's coffee table.

Is that what concerns her? Is she finding herself drawn to Christ — and afraid that her brother will be upset? Abe was truly ecumenical, respecting the beliefs of others, and he often liked to muse over the ways their faiths drew on each other. But still . . .

Sophie's teakettle whistled.

Gracie sipped her tea. "This is unusual! Peach?" Sophie didn't know Gracie's taste ran to the more prosaically comforting orange pekoe.

"And passion fruit. Sounds a bit sinful, doesn't it?" She laughed.

Gracie replied thoughtfully, "We have passion for all kinds of things. Causes. Our work — if we're fortunate."

"There have been times I'd hoped that Abe would be less passionate about the Deli."

And move south, Gracie knew.

"But I've given up."

Is this it, Lord? That she despairs of having him spend winters near her? But she indicated that she feared his disappointment in her — not hers in him.

"And it's nice to be here for Hanukkah."

"He was delighted to hear you were coming!"

Sophie frowned. "I wonder if he's delighted now."

Gracie caught her breath.

"I've been so moody. The poor man has enough to do without worrying about me."

She looked rueful.

Gracie murmured, "I'm sure he's just concerned."

Sophie sighed deeply. "Not — you think — disappointed? At least not yet?"

Gracie reminded her, "We were going to keep to less difficult topics, remember?"

Sophie nodded. Wriggling in her chair, she kicked off her shoes and tucked her stockinged legs beneath her. "I feel like I'm at camp again, a teenager."

"Except that now we won't be discussing boys!"

Mischievously, Sophie proposed, "Maybe Rocky?" She sobered. "But that's no joking matter, is it?"

"Nor is it serious. Rocky and I are just very good friends. He lost his wife, I lost my husband. That forges a human bond that needs no other reason for being."

"Shared pain. I wonder, is there any stronger adhesive than that to hold two people together?"

"There's love," Gracie said simply.

Softly, Sophie repeated, "Love." For a moment she seemed so far away, a tiny smile playing on her lips, her expression dreamy, that Gracie reconsidered Uncle Miltie's diagnosis.

Could it be, Lord? Is there a romantic inter-

*est in her life? But Abe wouldn't mind that . . .
would he?*

Maybe the Lord would give her a clue
soon — if He thought it was any of her business.

By the time Gracie said good-bye, she had
discussed with Sophie the best ways to use
up leftover pot roast, the annual rainfall in
southern Florida, her niece Carter's latest
promotion and the choir's upcoming cantata.

But she was no wiser about what was
troubling her friend when she left than she'd
been when she arrived.

While Gracie was still on the porch, brushing snow from her boots, she sniffed appreciatively the spicy aroma of garlic bread
wafting from her very own kitchen.

Dear Uncle Miltie!

"You spoil me!" she exclaimed. "I'm ravenous!"

"Well, if you insist on keeping your special
winter pesto around, how can I resist using
it?" He waggled a bushy eyebrow at her.

"But I need to cook the pasta still." He
checked the clock, as he pitched linguine
strands into a waiting pot of boiling water.

Gracie began to throw together a hasty
salad: shredded romaine lettuce, a handful

115

of chopped red cabbage, a shredded carrot, a last smidgeon of onion and a few stuffed olives, sliced.

Uncle Miltie tested a strand of linguine to see if it was done. "Seems ready. Let's sit down."

As if on cue, the kitchen door rattled.

"Let me guess," he said drily. "Marge."

It was Rocky.

Marge arrived five minutes later. They had just joined hands for grace when there came an unexpected knock.

Uncle Miltie guessed, "Pastor Paul."

It didn't take Hercule Poirot, Gracie thought to herself, to make the proper deduction. Their minister was the third of their regular trio of "uninvited" dinner guests.

His blond hair was slicked with melting snow.

"Brrr!" He stomped his feet.

"Sit," Uncle Miltie commanded. The young pastor hung up his coat and obeyed, then led them in giving thanks. They all dug in, with Rocky smacking his lips the loudest.

"Who's for seconds?" Uncle Miltie demanded. "I don't even need to ask you, Gravino. And Pastor Paul, well, riding a bike around in the snow's got to give a fellow an appetite."

Paul blushed. "Uncle Miltie, Gracie," he began, "I can't thank you enough for your boundless hospitality. At least one of you has a name that goes to the heart of your true nature."

Uncle Miltie preened.

"Not *you,*" Marge told him.

"What's the matter? Didn't you know that George Morgan meant 'master chef' and 'all-around great guy' in ancient Greek?"

"It's certainly Greek to me," Rocky replied. "But in plain old American, I'd like some more . . . please!"

They all laughed, as Gracie got up and went to the counter to replenish the salad bowl.

14

"I don't know what you did, Gracie." Abe set mugs of fresh coffee before Gracie and Uncle Miltie. "But Sophie seems more herself again. Your visit cleared something that was in the air, I just still don't know what."

"Men can't handle it when women are upset," Uncle Miltie said. "When my Doris was alive, I could stand anything but that."

"You're just an old softie, and that proves you were once a young softie," his niece told him fondly.

He looked at her tenderly, proving her point. Then he snorted.

"Listen to me, Abe. I'm going to tell you," he paused, "what I've already told Gracie."

"And that is . . . ?"

"Your sister's in love."

"Sophie —" Abe paled slightly. "— in love again, after all these years? And you . . . you've said this before?"

118

"Well," Uncle Miltie admitted, "Gracie rejected my theory."

"And so do I!" Abe shook his head.

Uncle Miltie leaned forward, elbows on the table. "Male intuition — trust me."

Abe shook his head.

"Like one of your stories," Uncle Miltie said. "You string all the non-related stuff together, but at the end it sort of makes sense."

"When there *is* an ending!" Rocky, just arriving, slid into the seat nearest Gracie.

Abe chose to ignore him. "Gracie, what's your take on Sophie?" he asked.

While Gracie considered, he puzzled, "But if she is in love — who's the lucky man?"

Uncle Miltie suggested, "Somebody in Florida?"

"But . . . why doesn't she just marry him and bring him home? Or bring him home and marry him — whichever. Would it help if I offered to throw a reception?" He looked to Gracie. "I guess from your expression — not."

"It's just — we're not certain yet."

"I'm certain!" Uncle Miltie declared.

"But it's better to wait —"

"— until she's ready," Abe finished. "As always, you're right."

"How's the pastrami today?" Rocky asked,

then broke off at Abe's expression. "I feel another story coming!"

Uncle Miltie asked, "Does this one have an ending?"

"I won't know until I get there." Abe's eyes twinkled.

"Do you want to order before or after?" Gracie reminded Rocky. "A couple of extra pickles and it won't matter if Abe goes into overtime. . . ."

Abe smiled at her. "There once was a young queen," he began.

"— in a very far country," Rocky chanted.

"— in a very far country."

Uncle Miltie asked, "How did you know that?"

Gracie laughed. "Abe's stories always happen in one far country or another."

"So reporters have a hard time checking his facts." Rocky grinned.

"This young queen was perfect. She had flawless beauty, impeccable manners, infallible intuition and such great knowledge that her tutors now came to learn from her. If she failed to clean her plate, the chief cook burned that particular recipe. If she covered her ears when a bird sang on her garden fence, it immediately threw itself from a precipice. And her garden, of course, was perfect."

"No weeds," Uncle Miltie said.

Rocky contributed, "No nasty grubs —"

"— or thistles."

"No dying leaves —"

"— or Japanese beetles —"

"or blight, drought, or frost —"

"Enough," Abe growled.

Looking pleased with themselves, Rocky and Uncle Miltie saluted one another. Then they exchanged high fives.

Abe ignored them.

"There was only one thing that marred the young queen's happiness. She was sick to death of being perfect. Perfection, she found, is —" he paused, indicating that Rocky and Uncle Miltie should fill in the blank.

Obligingly, they chorused, "Bor-ing!"

"Exactly. And she was certain that others found her as uninteresting as she herself did. Even her courtiers, who idolized her, seldom stopped to chat. The people of her kingdom sang her praises continually — but visited only when business demanded. And the castle cats yawned widely whenever she appeared.

"Only once did she give a royal ball. Those few who attended left early, pleading everything from sudden tennis elbow to an expected crisis at home.

"Day after day, she paused before one of the many castle mirrors and glowered at herself. Perhaps if a frown formed, it would mar her perfect beauty. But despite the ferocity of her glowering, no frown would cooperate. Well, she might not be able to change her appearance, but she could control her manners! At dinner that evening, she messily slurped her green pea soup. For a moment, her courtiers seemed perplexed, but soon all were happily slurping, dripping enough green spots to their clothing to equal hers. They applauded her inventiveness in designing such a pleasurable way to consume soup, and lavishly complimented the altered pattern of her splattered bodice.

" 'Such artistry!' cooed one prim lady. 'I shall certainly demand that my dressmaker imitate it precisely!' Taking her napkin, she used her fork tine as a quill to note the exact distribution of green spots.

"The princess sank more deeply into despair. No matter what she tried, her subjects named it perfection. When she deliberately stepped on her train and fell tumbling down the palace stairs, all of her staff chose that method of moving from one floor to another. When she savagely ripped the petals from her roses, almost at once, all the gardens of the kingdom were similarly denuded. 'Our princess is incapable of wrong,' they asserted. 'Why did we never realize how much more beautiful the flowers are without their petals?'

" 'It's no use. No use. No use . . .' One day the princess rocked back and forth on the railing of her balcony. 'I am doomed to odious perfection.' " Abe paused, sipping ice water.

"You always do that," Rocky accused, "leave us hanging."

"Only until my vocal chords have a moment of rest."

"Or until you think up an ending for your rambling!"

"Well. It seems a bit unseemly, perhaps, for us to engage in mirth while our poor young queen wallows in the despair of her affliction. Eventually her counselors recognized that she was miserable — *perfectly* miserable, of course. And since they truly cared for her, they cast about for a solution, an alleviation of her distress. And because the counselors were men, and men tread fearfully where emotional women are concerned, they decided that the only sensible solution was to find her a prince as perfect as she.

"This was no small task, as you can imagine — and if I were to recount the numerous hazards of their perilous journeys — how many were eaten by wild animals, how many lost forever in tangled forest — your sadness would equal that of the princess. Each day, she sat above the moat and increased its depth with her tears. Whenever a mounted messenger approached — or even a ragged beggar — her heart beat with renewed hope. Since it was obvious that she could not shed her own perfection, had they at last found someone who bore an equal burden?

"And then at last, one dew-drenched morning the princess heard the glad sound of trumpets — a bit out of tune, but she was able to ignore that slight imperfection, since they heralded grand news. She asked her maids to dress her hair — which had been perfectly beautiful even in its tumbled state — and wearing an elegant gown and a small, uncertain smile, she descended the curved marble stairway to see who awaited her.

"He was perfectly handsome, perfectly groomed, with perfect manners. His black boots were polished to an ebony sheen — so dustless the princess wondered if his groomsmen might have carried him from the roadway to the foyer. When he smiled his perfect smile, his perfect white teeth gleamed. He bowed with perfect grace, and presented her with one perfect rose. 'It was most difficult to find,' he admitted. 'It seems that nearly all of the roses in your kingdom have moulted!'

"After a brief courtship, the two married. The ceremony was conducted without flaw under perfect skies, while skilled harpists played without error."

"And they lived happily ever after?" Uncle Miltie asked.

"On the contrary. They made one another perfectly miserable! A little imperfection is what makes a relationship . . . perfect." He pushed back from the table. "Rocky, my friend, you were asking about the pastrami — it's —"

"— perfectly delicious?" Rocky asked. "No thank you. Give me the corned beef!"

It was only then that Gracie noticed Sophie, standing in the kitchen door holding a dripping ladle of which she seemed totally unaware. Her eyes were stricken.

Concerned, Gracie moved to her.

"Oh, Gracie!" Sophie moaned from the shelter of Gracie's embrace. "However did he find out?"

15

Gracie glanced at the clock and gasped. She was going to be late for cantata practice, and the scones for the following afternoon's holiday tea at Cordelia Fountain's Tourist Home were still not ready to go. Shaking out her apron, she glanced into the living room, where Gooseberry and Uncle Miltie half-dozed, half-watched an old western movie.

There was no hope for it. "Uncle Miltie." She shook him gently.

"They . . ." he mumbled, ". . . sure knew how . . . make movies back. . . ."

"Uncle Miltie, I hate to ask you —"

Gooseberry yawned and leapt to the floor, ready for action.

"Sorry." Gracie rubbed behind his ears, and he pushed into her hand. "You're a brilliant cat, but you don't know how to use oven mitts. At least not yet." Again, she spoke near her uncle's ear. "Uncle Miltie,

126

dear. . . ."

He roused, rubbed his eyes and muttered, "Just about fell asleep there, for a minute."

She explained how to tell when the scones were done. Then she asked, "You're sure . . . you don't mind?" She had almost asked if he were awake enough to handle it — but knew that he'd be insulted. After all, in his mind, he hadn't really dropped off.

"Happy to, Gracie. Now you just run along and do . . . whatever it is you're going to do."

"Cantata practice."

"I knew that." He made a third try to get up, but shook his head when she reached to steady him. "Run along, or you'll be late."

She was already late.

And Barb Jennings had little patience with tardiness.

That particular evening, however, she was nearly too busy to notice. The pageant participants were milling and jostling, two of the fourth-grade boys wrestling on the stage, putting the makeshift stable in jeopardy. A tiny tot was tugging at Barb's leg; fortunately, she was too distracted to notice. Three angels — not in full costume yet, but wearing their halos, were conducting themselves with what could only be termed an unangelic excess of energy.

Barb gasped, "Oh, Gracie, you're here! Praise be! Can you please keep me from having a total breakdown and help Comfort and Linda — and the others? I'm wondering if we'll ever be able to bring this thing together!"

Gracie hurried over to the source of the bedlam. Even Don Delano rolled his eyes. "Just think," he whispered to Gracie, "in a few years they'll be in my science lab!"

"By then," she promised, "they'll have matured —"

"— or I'll have taken early retirement!"

"Boys and girls!" Gracie pleaded.

"Oh, Mrs. Parks! Did you bring cookies? Did you bring Gooseberry? Where's Mr. Morgan?"

The sound and gymnastics had accelerated, rather than diminishing.

"Oh, for goodness sake!" Estelle descended now and made herself known. "Have you no respect — for God, if for no one else! What do you suppose He thinks of these shenanigans — in His own house!"

Silence fell. But it was a quiet born of fear — even resentment — rather than the respect Estelle demanded. Cowed, eyes downcast, the children sank either into the front pew or onto the floor.

And suddenly Gracie yearned for the

noise. It, at least, had been joyous.

"There!" Estelle elevated her nose as she returned to her place in the choir loft.

Gracie decided to keep her thoughts to herself — but Patsy Clayton spoke up decisively.

"Why are you so mean, Miss Livett?" she demanded. "I think you must be very unhappy."

Estelle, Gracie was sad to see, ignored her. At least, Gracie comforted herself, she was keeping her word and seeing the cantata through, despite her resentments. Still, Patsy was right to sense them under the surface.

The practice proceeded smoothly, and only Patsy seemed somewhere far away. After her outburst, she went through her paces with emotionless accuracy.

In the choir loft, a subdued Estelle had accepted her small solo assignment with apparent humility. Her expression, however, was stolid, her eyes guarded.

Gracie decided to listen to the music with her heart and not just with her ears. She needed, if only for an instant, to put away her concerns about Estelle, and about Patsy, too. Each stanza began in the lower ranges — but with each succeeding phrase as-

cended the scale in an acceleration that
spoke of awe.

Day had dimmed.
The sun had set.
The night was quiet, and yet . . .
And yet . . .
A sense of deep expectancy
Stirred in the hillside's rocky lea,
As shepherds watched their flocks by
    night . . .
    And angels moved
    In unseen flight!

The pageant shepherds were in position
— some curled in feigned slumber, others
bored but watchful. Pastor Paul, working
the overhead — which also served as spotlight — projected a night sky, sweeping over
the hillside in alternating shadow and dim
light.

A star expanded —
Vibrant!
Bright!
The clouds,
Enveloped in its light,
Took on the shape of angel throngs.
The starlight thrummed with unheard
    songs.

Fear formed itself,
Cut like a sword —
   And angels struck
   The opening chord!

Barb gave the signal for the most intricate of the choir numbers — an entanglement of *"Glorias"* — at times exultant, trumpeting, triumphant — at others softened by wonder, becoming a melodic lullaby. The youth praise band echoed the mood in sections — brass, percussion, flute — while Pastor Paul set the stage dancing with spots of brilliant light.

The number closed to silence.

"Wow!" Patsy's widened eyes shone. "Do you s'pose it really sounded like that?" Gracie's heart leaped to see the glow on her face.

Thank You, Lord.

But then the little girl breathed a deep sigh. " 'Course not," she whispered, slumping again.

"Fantastic practice!" Barb beamed on all of them. "You're wonderful, every one of you!" To Gracie, it seemed that she favored Estelle with a particularly warm smile.

And well-deserved, Gracie thought, planning to add her own congratulations. She had sung especially beautifully. But Estelle

131

once again donned her mantle of conde-scension.

"Scarcely fantastic," she muttered as she reached Gracie, "though not bad for a small-town, untrained choir."

Lord, forgive me. I know Estelle's Your child, but she can be so infuriating! I don't think there's any changing her, although You'd know that best. So I guess I'll have to ask that You grant us triple doses of forbearance.

"Mrs. Parks, are you praying, or is the light just hurting your eyes?"

Gracie eased into the pew beside Patsy. "It's pretty bright, isn't it?" she hedged.

Patsy sighed. "I'm sure glad I didn't inter-rupt you and God!" She frowned. "That is, if —"

There really is one? Gracie finished in her thoughts. "Oh, Patsy, dear —"

"But what I really needed to ask you this time is — why is Miss Livett so . . . so . . . so —" Again, she sighed.

Gracie patted the small hand. "I just don't know, dear. Perhaps she's lonely."

"I hate to see anyone sad."

"I know, dear. Especially at Christmas-time."

Patsy withdrew her hand. "Especially at any time! I was wondering . . . if it's only that she's lonely . . . I could go visit her."

Dear Lord, this sweet, sweet child!

"Because I'd be glad to. In fact," she stood, catching her small folded walker, "that's 'zactly what I'm going to do!"

16

If anyone in Willow Bend — or Mason City, for that matter — knew how to throw a gala pre-Christmas tea, it was Cordelia Fountain.

Her establishment, the town's only tourist home, with its nineteenth-century splendor, lent itself to such celebration. Alterations dating to the late Victorian era only increased its charm. Cupolas, gables adorned with ornate gingerbread, a gazebo — all added to its picture-postcard look.

Cordelia frequently called Rocky Gravino with ideas for newspaper stories featuring her historic residence. She pestered him so often, in fact, that more than once he confided his frustration to Gracie. "Any day now, she'll call to report an infestation of historic bats in the attic. If everyone in Mason County demanded the space both Cordelia and Tom Ritter expect, the *Gazette* would wind up heavier than a couple of encyclopedia volumes!"

"Cordelia's great for Willow Bend! Her quest for perpetual publicity is bound to affect local tourism! And isn't it a part of your job to give Willow Bend a positive image? The Ewing farm's fields of sunflowers —"

"Now that," he agreed, "was a nice little feature piece!"

It certainly had been! Gracie envisioned the half-page color photo of acres and acres of sunflower heads, all facing the same direction, and — surrounded and all but submerged — Clancy Ewing — wearing a huge straw hat and a giant smile. Strangers might find the pose quaint, but to Willow Benders the Ewings were up-to-the-moment organic farmers with a growing business.

"And you always give great reports on the church and school events — plays, concerts, science projects —"

"Don't forget," he told her dryly, "I cover the news. I'm actually not in the promotion business."

"You're keeping Willow Bend on its toes," she agreed. "Some of the time, anyway."

For the event, Cordelia Fountain had selected the *crème de la crème* not only of Willow Bend's society, but of Mason City's, too. Gracie couldn't help wondering amusedly if she or any of her helpers would have even known about the tea if they were not catering. Don't be petty, she cautioned herself.

As they bustled about, her crew repeatedly paused to exclaim over Cordelia's display of exquisitely crafted and rare ornaments.

"Oh, Gracie!" Marge exclaimed. "Those are so gorgeous! I'd love to have carved wooden snowflakes like that in my shop!"

Gracie, meanwhile, was admiring the magic Cordelia had worked with fresh pine cones, swatches of brocade and gold spray paint. Garlands and rich, heavyweight satin ribbons festooned the staircase and railings, while red and white poinsettias blossomed out of antique Chinese cachepots.

Suddenly, the Turner twins appeared.

"Those are teaberries — aren't they?" Tyne looked closely at a garland.

"Or partridge berries —"

"— or berries from dogwood? I never can —"

"— tell the difference, can any of you?"

"Let's worry about it later," Barb told them. "We've got to get this show *off* the road and into Cordelia's kitchen. Right now!"

"Vvrrooom!" The twins, rezipping their parkas, headed straight back out to the van

for another load. As the door closed behind them, a chill wind snaked in. Candle flames bent, flickered, then resumed their steady glow until the door opened once again, admitting the twins and large trays of petit fours.

If Cordelia's Christmas decor was practically over-the-top, the outfit worn by Sherry Ritter, the mayor's wife, truly was! Her dress was made of deep red velvet, with a high collar and inset lace panels. Her earrings dangled to her shoulders, around which she wore a kind of green boa. She wore a corsage of holly and red roses on her left wrist.

Suddenly Cordelia salied into the kitchen, obviously quite pleased with herself. "Have you seen Mr. Gravino anywhere?"

"Mr. Gravino," thought Gracie. He was Rocky to everyone — even Cordelia, in normal circumstances. But such special occasions required formality, she understood.

Marge was the first to answer. "Mr. Gravino hasn't yet arrived," she told Cordelia, giving an extra emphasis to the unfamiliar "Mister."

"*Mmm,*" Cordelia murmured. She turned to Gracie. "If you see him, please tell him where to find me. We'll expect to serve in fifteen minutes."

In the act of leaving, she turned, her expression suddenly concerned. "Oh, Gracie," she whispered. "You would tell me, wouldn't you, if I were making a fool of myself?"

You have to love her, Gracie thought, and I do. If Willow Bend didn't have such characters, I'm sure I'd have to invent them!

Rocky arrived shortly, carrying his notepad. "Ben's on his way," he told Gracie, referring to Ben Tomlinson, the *Gazette*'s most stalwart photographer.

Now he scanned the crowd. "She's not here, is she?"

"Your biggest fan?" teased Marge. "The one who hails you as her hero?"

He glared at her.

"If she is, I haven't seen her —" Gracie broke off, for as if answering a curtain call, Maria Carlotta Estalena Lucia Buonarotti descended the staircase leading to the drawing room. She paused halfway to nod to a waiting harpist. The first melodic strumming quieted the assemblage.

In contrast to the guests, and to her own customary flamboyant style, Maria was dressed simply in a classic white toga and gold strap sandals, their rich color echoed

138

only in a gleaming band high on her left arm and a narrow ribbon, woven into her thick single braid.

Ben appeared at the edge of the crowd; a flashbulb popped.

Then came the glorious music — and with what seeming effortlessness! *Thank You, Lord, for the gift of this woman's voice!*

When her recital ended, Maria bowed to the applause and strode purposefully across the room.

Rocky took a deep breath. Panic seeped through his composure. He licked his lips nervously and cracked his knuckles.

"Not to fear, Rocco Gravino," Maria reassured him. "Only let me gaze on you — for mere moments — and recall those sweet memories of my childhood."

Rocky relaxed, just a little.

"You will not reject my adoration, I hope. I mean no harm." When Rocky found no ready reply, she cupped his face gently in her long, expressive hands. "You must tell me, one day, what you know of my friend Rocco? News of your uncle would give me great gratitude."

Rocky cleared his throat.

"You will do this?"

"I know only a little —"

"But even a tiny amount will increase my

meager knowledge."

Rocky cleared his throat. "I may be able to find an old photo —"

"*Ah!*" Maria caught him to her in an enveloping hug. "A photo! To see him again —" Her voice broke, and, backing away, she caught her hands to her breast. "Forgive. I am forget my promises. Too impetuous, but also too excited! Excuse, please."

With that apology, she turned and left them. Rocky righted his tie. Not quite meeting Gracie's glance, he said respectfully, "She's . . . pretty intense, isn't she? Uncle Rocco might have been wise to take notice."

17

How wonderful to be here in my own cozy kitchen! Thank You, Lord, for the gift of it! She pressed her fingertips to her throbbing temple.

"Headache, Gracie?" Uncle Miltie led her to an overstuffed chair and stood behind it. "Let me treat you to the Morgan sure-fire cure."

His arthritic fingers were still nimble enough to massage her neck gently, then her shoulders. Gradually, her tension eased. "You're wonderful," she said.

"I know." She could sense his loving smile. "I guess that makes us both lucky."

Her eyelids drooped. She felt herself slipping into drowsiness. A furry head pushed itself into her grasp. Good old Gooseberry. He could always tell when she needed comforting. Or was it he who needed it? With a soft thud he was in her lap, licking at her chin. She laughed, and suddenly felt energized.

Gooseberry could always tell, too, when she needed to be up and about her work.

"We could eat at Abe's," Uncle Miltie suggested. "My treat."

She kissed his cheek. "You're sweet. But I'd never make it. I'd find a nice soft pile of snow and take a nap." Somehow she hadn't yet stood up.

His face mirrored concern. "Then I'll get us a little soup. With cheese and crackers. You and Gooseberry rest there." As he turned, he commented, "It's all those airs people were putting on at Cordelia's — breathing them can be a little toxic."

Gracie closed her eyes again. Maybe he was right. But when you came right down to it, they were all just honest folks like her and Uncle Miltie — honest, if a little hoity-toity.

During the night, it snowed three inches — the kind of accumulation Gracie loved. Replacing her walking shoes with fur-lined boots, she set off, Gooseberry pouncing ahead to draw an erratic pattern of paw-prints and tummy slides across the pristine surface.

Gracie knew how he felt. There was such a sensation of power — primal, perhaps —

142

to be the first to track across such whiteness. Who could resist?

When El was alive and Arlen off at school, the two of them — three, once Gooseberry came into their lives as a bumbling kitten — loved to walk on such a morning. No need for inspirational tapes then. Praise was the state of their mutual being.

Each bush they came upon was clotted with pure whiteness; each fence-post wore a rounded cap of purity. Snow piled on each limb, from massive branch to tiny twig — and remained there until some scant movement of bird or breeze stirred and sent it falling in fragments.

Oh, how I miss that sweet man, Lord!

But El was with God now — as were El's parents and hers, Aunt Doris, and so many other dear departed ones. *We never got to say good-bye, Lord. The accident took him so quickly. . . .*

"You understand, don't you, Goosie, my love?" She bent to stroke his arching back. His purring was a tiny motor, and his fur was in bright orange contrast to the prevailing whiteness.

He would have stood there, pressing his head into her mittened hand, for hours. "But we have things to do," she said. "Well, at least I do. Uncle Miltie and I plan to put up the tree when I get back — and what fun you'll have then, batting at balls and lights."

And when the presents were wrapped and placed, he would circle endlessly, nudging, sniffing.

"Or are you grown beyond that, boy? Too mature to show curiosity?"

She knew better. When he had tired of exploration, he'd curl up beneath the tree and take a nap — that is until the aromas of her Christmas baking roused him to wakefulness, and the expectation he might have a creamy dish to lick.

The only section of Willow Run Road that gave Gracie — and Gooseberry — pause was shortly past the bridge, where — deep within a vast stand of pines and hemlocks — Trevel Landry had long ago built a log cabin for himself and his intended wife.

A whole mythology had developed around this rarely glimpsed citizen of Willow Bend, now in his early seventies, and the intended bride who had died two nights before their wedding date. Gracie had never seen her, but El had wryly described her as a young woman who had somehow become a great beauty only after her death. But there was nothing exaggerated about Trevel Landry's possessiveness, her husband had said. The man had built the cabin as a kind of hermitage, a way to keep her all to himself.

That Landry had buried his bride-to-be near the cabin and surrounded her grave and monument with a high fence gave some credence to at least some of the rumors. But what troubled Gracie — and Gooseberry — were his dogs, all of mixed breed and malicious temperament. When they were chained, they expressed their ill will with leaps and snarls, made all the more aggressive by the prospect of a large orange cat sauntering anywhere near their territory.

But when the dogs were loose — especially if Landry was not at home to order them back — that was a different story.

His one-way tracks in the new snow showed that he was away this particular morning.

And the dogs *were* loose.

Heart pounding with a quick prayer, Gracie picked up a large fallen branch and backed slowly along the roadway. Gooseberry suddenly was gone, leaving her to her own defense. Fortunately the dogs knew the boundaries of their property, and if Gracie respected those, she believed — she hoped — she'd be safe.

She would have been but for one, smaller

than the others, who seemed to think he had something to prove through bravado. Close and closer he came, hunched, tail down, bristles up and every tooth in his mouth showing in a stiffened evil grin. When he stepped onto the roadway itself, Gracie tightened her hold on the branch. Her prayer accelerated.

Just when it seemed she could almost feel the dog's hot breath, when she could see his haunches bunched for a leap, a harsh voice called out. "Caesar! Here!"

Gracie exhaled relief. Cowering, whining, its tail flicking, the dog crawled toward Landry, who kicked it savagely and sent it yipping homeward.

Then Landry himself strolled toward Gracie, his expression no less hostile than Caesar's. "You got no business here, lady."

He was carrying something — something large and wooden, brightly colored like a lawn decoration, but broken.

He looked down at it, then at her. "You tell anyone you seen this, I'll sic Caesar on you for sure."

He turned and walked away, and the other dogs followed meekly.

She hadn't planned to walk as far as the church, but she knew she would welcome its calmness. No one had been through the front door yet since the new snowfall. As she often did, she grieved the modern necessity of locked churches. *What possessions are we guarding, Lord? The collection plates? Hymnals? Communion set? Barb's wonderful brass music stand? All expendable, in the eternal view.*

Breeze stirred the pines, dislodging small avalanches. A squirrel loped across the lawn, leaving his own distinct pattern. Joining her, now that danger was past, and knowing his duty, Gooseberry streaked toward him, and the squirrel accelerated his pace, his tiny feet skidding as he scurried up the trunk and onto a low branch. From that safe distance, he shrilly lectured Gooseberry, who paid not the slightest attention.

Gracie walked around the church. The moment she noticed that the snow there had been disturbed, she registered the sound of a piano. What she heard were tentative notes, flawed and repeated. Still, Gracie thought she recognized the hymn — "In the Bleak Midwinter." Appropriate, she thought, skimming the lyrics through her mind. "Snow on snow. . . ." Such a somber tune, though — so in contrast with the joyous Christmas melodies heard more often — yet with that poignancy that distinguished Christina Rossetti's poetry.

Another sour note. Who could it be? Possibly a child?

And then she heard voices. Or — a single voice?

Creeping closer, she eased the door open.

"I really, really, really want to believe! I truly do! Isn't there some way You could send me a sign — You did for Gideon, 'member? And Moses? And Noah with the rainbow . . . and lots and lots others. Maybe not kids like me — but I really don't think I can wait until I grow up to know for sure."

Patsy. Her voice murmured on, rising and falling. Pleading.

Gracie paused, then backed away, pulling the door to behind her.

I have no right to intrude, she told the Lord. *I'll leave the two of you alone. But if I could make a request — please, oh, please, do give her the sign she requires.*

When Gracie reached home, she entered the kitchen in time to hear something heavy thumping down the stairs from the attic.

Her heart jolted, her own terrors of the morning forgotten. *Oh, dear Lord, please — not Uncle Miltie!*

18

Uncle Miltie stood — rubbing his right hip — among a welter of bags and boxes.

"It was the Christmas tree threw me." He gave a halfhearted kick at the long narrow box, still bearing the price tag from seven years earlier.

El and I bought it together, remember, Lord? It was El who decided we should go to artificial, confessing sheepishly he was getting too old to scramble through the woods and drag home a real tree.

That first year, she had so ached for the scent of new evergreen boughs that El had bought pine-scented air freshener, spraying it liberally several times a day. She had decided his extra effort was worth her acceptance. Artificial it was, then.

"Uncle Miltie, dear — are you hurt?"

He shook his head, then grimaced and limped to a chair. "Maybe a little." He pushed at a clutter of decorations that had spilled from tipped boxes. "Hope none of them got broke."

She laid an arm across his shoulder. "The important thing is that you're still in one piece!"

He chuckled, "I've yet to see a plaster cast on a Christmas ball." More seriously he added, "I know how precious some of those are to you, Gracie. They bring back such memories and all."

Dear man, could he even guess how precious he himself was to her? Shrugging out of her jacket, telling herself that if the boots dripped, so much the better — it would give her a start on mopping — she knelt to reclaim the boxes and their contents.

Gooseberry "helped" — sniffing, pushing bright globes with his paw.

One decoration was broken — a glass bell, lavender and pink, bought by her parents for their first tree together.

Oh, well.

Making certain that she blocked Uncle Miltie's view, she carefully gathered the fragments and put them in the corner of a box. She'd throw them out later, when he was napping or watching TV.

He cleared his throat. "Any broken?"

"Everything's fine," she assured him.

He sighed deeply. "That's a relief."

150

She crossed her fingers where he couldn't see them. *Lord, please forgive me for this teeny-tiny white lie.*

It was an incredibly busy day.

Although both Uncle Miltie and Gooseberry tried to assist with the assembly and decorating of the tree, one was always underfoot, and the other had injured himself more than had at first been apparent.

When at last it was done to everyone's satisfaction — some low inexpensive balls for Gooseberry's pleasure, a plethora of tinsel and icicles to please Uncle Miltie, and enough memory-tinged decorations to satisfy Gracie — the empty boxes were ready to be taken upstairs until after New Year's.

Uncle Miltie yawned. "Leave 'em for me, Gracie dear."

She made no answer, but determined that as soon as he began to snore, she'd take them up herself. His neck and limbs were too precious to face harm a second time that day.

Then came the baking. She had determined to cram in as much as possible before a late lunch, then take tins around to a few special neighbors and friends. Included in those so favored would be her current objects of worry, Estelle and Sophie. She'd fix a special colorful tin for Patsy later.

The kitchen filled quickly with the aromas of cinnamon, lemon, vanilla, peppermint and melting chocolate.

Gracie felt enclosed in warmth, both physical and emotional. *This is my true home, she told the Lord. Dare I hope that Heaven will smell like baking day?*

The timer let out a shrill ping. Just as Gracie bent to remove a pan of cinnamon stars, the door rattled, and Marge entered.

"You really should leave your door open, Gracie." She draped her jacket over a chair and slipped her feet out of her boots. "You'd tempt the entire neighborhood! There'd be a mass raid organized on your kitchen — make cookie rustlers out of otherwise law-abiding citizens!"

Gracie offered a plate of peppermint chocolate drops. "These are cool enough."

Marge reached, drew back, asked, "Are you sure, Gracie?" and took one before Gracie could answer.

"I was going to bring a plate over later anyway."

"You're the best!" Marge closed her eyes and breathed ecstatically. "*Yum* and *yum* again!"

While Gracie continued to work, Marge

continued to sample. "I see you have your tree up." She paused for a bite of ginger-snap before saying, "Maybe I'll find time by New Year's. Think?"

They laughed companionably.

From the living room, the television murmured, not exactly proving that Uncle Miltie was awake, but at least that the Cartwrights were once again making the West safe for women and children, if only in reruns.

"I wonder how many times he's watched that episode?" Marge smiled. "Does he think it might end differently this time?"

"I heard that!" Uncle Miltie called, startling both of them.

Marge glared accusingly in his direction. "He certainly has good hearing for someone his age!"

"Heard that, too!"

Marge grabbed another cookie, a walnut-spice wafer this time.

There was no further response from the living room.

"You know what I like best about Christmas, Gracie? Besides the goodies, that is." She tested a gumdrop cookie for coolness and tried it. "Caroling. Lights shining on fresh snow. The crisp air and the tingling on your face. Everyone singing their hearts out

153

— whether they're in perfect pitch or not. Just the whole wonderful experience — and people so obviously joyful. I can't wait!"

"You're right, Marge, dear," Gracie agreed. Then she said gently, "But don't forget our Lord when you make your list. We're singing our hearts out for Him."

Marge took her tin of cookies home with her, and Gracie set off with as many as a sturdy canvas tote bag could handle. First, she stopped at the Searfosses'. She had baked some sugarless brownies for Anna, whose diabetes forbade most sweets. Though Anna and Joe both urged her to stay, to visit "for a spell," she promised to come back soon, when holiday errands were behind her.

As she was leaving, she noticed their own little artificial tree was still untrimmed.

"We'll get to it soon," Joe said, noticing Gracie's gaze.

Anna added, "With my last eye surgery. . . ." Her devoted husband patted her shoulder softly.

"Have Christmas with us!" Gracie said, wondering why she hadn't thought of it before. "Arlen and his family aren't coming until after New Year's, but Carter plans to be here —"

"Dear Carter! How lovely it would be to see her again!"

It always twinged Gracie's heart when Anna spoke so casually of "seeing." She had been legally blind for years as a result of her diabetes. It was a tragedy, but one she had met with courage and fortitude.

"Is Carter still sending the bad guys to prison?" Joe asked.

Gracie nodded. "Still with the district attorney's office." She was very proud of her lawyer niece in Chicago, and everyone knew it.

"Such a little mite," Joe chuckled. "Hard to believe. Hard to believe. We do remember her in pigtails!"

"She'd love to see both of you. Please do join us!"

"Are you certain —" But Anna's mouth had curved into a smile. "We wouldn't want to put you out."

Joe said, "I could make myself useful. Carve the turkey, if you have one —"

"No one carves better than my Joe!" Anna's hand covered her husband's, still on her shoulder, and squeezed.

"But if it's not turkey —"

Gracie, who'd been vacillating between ham and goose, abandoned both then and there. "We're having turkey."

"What would Christmas dinner be without it?" Anna fairly twinkled. "I could bring my orange-cranberry relish, if you like, since Joe and I like to make it together. Three-bean salad, too."

"Lovely!" Gracie assured her. "Lovely and delicious! There can never be too much bounty, and leftovers are part of the pleasure, keeping us fed until New Year's."

"Oh, yes! Thank you, Gracie!"

Joe saw Gracie to the door. "Thank you, dear friend. You bring far more than cookies, whenever you come!"

Next, Gracie stopped by Sophie's quarters in Abe's house. Although she rapped several times, and she could hear at least one voice, no one came to the door.

Perhaps the television —

She knocked again, more loudly.

"Just a minute!" Sophie sang out and, with a telephone in one hand, she peered out the window and waved a welcome.

As the door opened, Gracie heard her say, "I wonder — could I call you back later?" A pause. "A friend dropped by." Another pause, then a whispered, "Me, too."

Her face was flushed as she turned from replacing the receiver — and her eyes were as bright as any Christmas light. "A friend," she explained unnecessarily.

156

"From Florida?"

For a moment, Sophie looked wary, then shrugged and nodded.

More and more, Gracie thought, I have to agree with Uncle Miltie. There's an active romance here.

"I know it's like taking ice cubes to Eskimos," she said, "but I brought a few cookies."

"Oh!" Sophie clapped her hands in child-like delight. "Anyone else's are always a treat!" Her expression suddenly clouded.

Gracie watched, but said nothing.

Sophie glanced toward the phone.

She doesn't want me to stay, Gracie thought. *She can't wait to get back to her conversation. Oh, how I want to ask —*

It was sometimes a struggle to rein in her curiosity — which could stand her in good stead where mysteries were concerned but could so easily be construed as nosiness in other situations. If Sophie had been depressed, Gracie would have plunged in. But her friend seemed cheerful in the extreme and so the right thing was to be discreet.

"Look," she protested, "I need to be going." And Sophie didn't try to stop her.

Lord, I should just be pleased that she's happy — at least at this moment.

She contained her natural curiosity somewhat by focusing on her last stop — at Estelle's. Perhaps Estelle, too, would have put aside her unhappiness.

She wouldn't be able to stay long, she was thinking as she hurried up the walk. Uncle Miltie — and Gooseberry — would surely be harboring hunger pangs. She smiled, thinking of them — of the warmth and unconditional love they contributed to her life. It wasn't the same as when El was alive, but nothing could ever match that happiness. Yet she was content. She had a blessed life.

Estelle's house was quiet. The porch had been swept recently, and no new snow had accumulated. Gracie stepped carefully, wanting to keep the tin of cookies upright.

There was no answer to her first knock. She tried again, and heard the sound of hurried footsteps and a quick, rhythmic thumping. She frowned. It sounded for all the world like Uncle Miltie's walker — though softer.

The door opened. Gracie, expecting to greet Estelle, had to drop her gaze by half.

"It's me, Mrs. Parks," Patsy Clayton chirped. " 'Member I told you I was going to visit? Me and Miss Livett are playing checkers — and I'm winning!"

"That's lovely, dear. Please give this gift

to Estelle for me." Gracie handed her the tin of cookies, which the girl juggled by maneuvering her walker with one hand. Gracie was about to leave when Patsy, eyes dancing, whispered, "Tell you a secret, Mrs. Parks?"

She beckoned, and Gracie bent down and offered an ear.

"I threw a sheepskin at God," she said quickly, turned, and shut the door.

Gracie was puzzled. A sheepskin? Whatever did the child mean? And why would she throw anything at God? Was this some new way of questioning His existence?

19

"She meant a fleece, of course, like Gideon!"

"So all's right with the world — for the moment." Uncle Miltie held out his plate for seconds. Gracie had prepared a simple meal — sweet sausage, green peppers, onions and red-skinned potatoes.

"One of my favorites," her uncle proclaimed.

She refrained from mentioning that he said that at nearly every meal, no matter the menu.

"Wonder why Rocky isn't here. Must be a deadly serious deadline! Oh, well," he grinned, "more for me!" He lifted a forkful. Then paused. "And our charming neighbor — she manage to cook her own dinner this time?"

"She stopped by for cookie-tasting earlier today."

"With a few insults thrown in, as I recall."

Once again, the fork paused. "She isn't sick, I hope."

Gracie teased, "Are you suggesting that my cookies — ?"

He ducked his head. "Never!"

"I think she may be decorating her tree. She said today that she hadn't managed to get it done yet."

"Almost too late."

Gracie half-closed her eyes in memory. Her own parents had put up the tree after the children were in bed Christmas Eve. Santa Claus got the credit, but it was her parents who were bone-weary.

Uncle Miltie said, "Ours looks real nice."

"Yes, it does."

Her economy-conscious parents had used only a few bought decorations — including that lovely, fragile bell — now broken. Ivory Soap flakes served as very satisfactory snow, while strings of popcorn, cranberries and dried fruit slices looped from branch to branch.

Uncle Miltie sopped up the remainder of his broth with buttered homemade bread. "Things were different then."

Gracie started. "You were reading my mind?"

"I recognize that 'long ago' look — and I was thinking back, too — how when I was a youngster, I felt rich if my stocking held a tissue-wrapped orange and one of those little cardboard boxes of candy. Ever see one? There was a white string handle — and the chocolate drops were the first to go."

Gracie smiled.

"And then, under the tree, one toy and some clothes. Oh, and always a book."

Quietly, Gracie went to fetch a plate of cookies.

He admired them extravagantly, then suggested, "They'd go mighty good with ice cream."

"You're spoiled," she teased, opening the freezer door.

"I know." He sighed, leaned back in his chair, and patted his stomach. "Ain't it grand?"

It's strange how time works, Lord. I think I have ages to get things done — and then, suddenly, WHAM!

Three days until Christmas! Only three days, seventy-two hours, some of which must be given over to the mundane act of sleeping.

Well, there was no better occasion than a prayer-walk for making mental lists. She certainly needed the Lord's help if she were to bake fifty dozen more cookies to fill orders and deliver to friends and shut-ins — all of whom required short visits. She also was expected to attend the cantata dress rehearsal — that would be tomorrow afternoon — and the performance itself that evening, after which she was in charge of refreshments. Then Christmas Eve would be given to caroling.

But this evening she was catering the Women's Club gift exchange. Though she had enough petit-fours in the freezer, she must make the ice ring punch, mold red and green mints in the shape of holly leaves, and prepare chocolate-almond bark. And after all this, there were groceries to buy for Christmas dinner, gifts to wrap —

She paused, sagging against a fence-post.

Lord, why do we do this to ourselves? Here it is, Christmas — the season in which we celebrate the most wonderful gift ever given. Why can't we just relax and joyously savor the wonder?

For the remainder of her walk, Gracie did just that.

Uncle Miltie looked down from the stepladder, planted firmly in the mulch blanketing her hydrangeas for the winter. "Figured I'd do a bit more decorating." He hung a few plastic hooks from the gutter before saying slyly, "seeing as how you and your favorite uncle will be helping to judge the contest."

"You're my only uncle," she began, smiling. Then, sharply, "contest? What contest?"

"Christmas decorations. Outdoors. Hand me that, will you?" He pointed to a string of stars.

She did. "I hadn't even heard of a contest!"

He snorted. "No one did. Not even His Honor himself — until he saw that Avery was having one. Guess he figured it'd ruin his shot at the White House if anybody got ahead of him. Still, the timing's way off," Uncle Miltie pointed out acidly. "A decoration contest should have been planned months ago!"

"And we're judging? When did this all come about?"

"Just now. When you were walking. Our esteemed mayor insisted that if you had time for hiking, you had time to 'serve your community.'"

From his inflection, she knew that the final three words were a direct quotation.

Despite the snow, she sank to the porch step. She had just been asking the Lord to help her slow down, to concentrate on the simplicity of that first Christmas miracle.

Descending cautiously, Uncle Miltie

164

placed a hand on her shoulder. "Gracie, I'm sorry."

She was feeling numb. Besieged. She couldn't deal with this, not another obligation. She just couldn't.

Or can I, Lord?

"It's just — that Ritter's such a steamroller. He kept hammering and hammering until I gave in."

She nodded, catching his hand in hers. "It's all right, Uncle Miltie."

"But it's *not* all right! You're worn to a frazzle, and instead of helping —" His voice shook.

"It's not your fault, Uncle Miltie. I know how Tom can be."

He brushed away snow and sat beside her. "Wouldn't surprise me if he hadn't waited until he'd seen you'd gone — knowing what a pushover I am." He sighed.

Something niggled at the edge of her memory — but she was too weary to pursue it. There was so much more to do!

She stood, brushing snow off the seat of her pants. Forcing her voice to lightness, she said, "Come to think of it, it might be fun! How else will we take the time to see and appreciate all the decorating Willow Bend has done to honor our Savior's birth?"

20

The Women's Club gift exchange was a pleasure for Gracie. Contrary to some popular opinions concerning such clubs, this group of Willow Bend ladies — many of them members of Eternal Hope Community Church — was committed to helping women in their worldwide struggles.

As president, Linda Cantrell spoke in the pine-fragrant, candlelit meeting place — so crowded with holiday gift bags and wrapped packages that there was scarcely room for stepping without getting tangled in curled ribbons.

"No matter how much we grieve for the near-slavery of some of our sisters in other nations, there's little we can do to free them." She looked around. "But we can send things that represent us and our loving support. . . ."

She gestured thoughtfully. "And so now, the moment we've all been waiting for! The gift exchange!"

It was like no other gift exchange Gracie had ever experienced. Comfort Harding, representing the women of African nations, wore an exotic animal print. Marge sat in for the women of Afghanistan; an old-fashioned hat-pin skewered a sheer black veil to her upswept hair, allowing it to drape across her face. Sherry Ritter had volunteered to be a proxy for the poor in India's streets. She wore a stunning blue and gold sari purchased on one of several trips abroad.

"Good will missions," she and the mayor insisted. "Forging political and economic liaisons between our fair city and foreign nations."

Uncle Miltie had observed caustically, "That way, it's tax deductible."

The Turner twins were "runners," delivering the gaily wrapped packages to the three women seated at a long, festively draped table. Barb was in charge of placing opened gifts in the proper pile for post-Christmas mailing through a Christian agency.

And what gifts there were! For India and Africa, there was clothing in every size from infant on up. For all three destinations, the Bible, *Guideposts* magazine and *Daily Guideposts* were gathered in appropriate translations, as well as cooking utensils, bedding, towels, nonperishable foodstuffs, toys, games, hand creams and baubles: bracelets, earrings and beads. Each gift — whether to nurture the body or the spirit — was greeted with appropriate *ooohs, ahhhs,* and applause.

How much better, Lord, than for each of us to carry home some semi-expensive bauble or gadget we don't need! Unbidden, tears came to Gracie's eyes. *Please bless each woman who receives a portion of this bounty — and in her secret heart may she realize that only through You do we give so generously.*

Gracie knew that some Willow Bend women — with this particular event in mind — saved pocket change throughout the year. *Lord, for those in this group who have genuinely sacrificed in their giving — please grant an extra measure of joy.* She murmured a silent "amen." It was time to serve refreshments.

The next morning, Gracie rose before dawn. It was essential if she were to have time for her walk — and she well knew that she required that spiritual refurbishing if she were survive the following few days.

Leaving Gooseberry still asleep, she chose

a familiar route through the sleeping town. Smoke curled lazily from chimney after chimney. Fresh snow lightly covered the crusting mounds deposited earlier from shoveled sidewalks and driveways, or plowed from the streets. The new sprinkling added a quality of mystery to strung bulbs and garlands, and also to the carolers, Nativity figures, Santas, Rudolphs — everything imaginable to represent both the secular and the sacred.

As she approached the Cantrell home, then the Claytons', she first pictured Amy sweetly asleep in her upstairs bedroom, then Patsy, next door. Dear, troubled Patsy — who had found excitement in "throwing a sheepskin at God." Was she, too, sleeping? Or did she lie awake, waiting for her fleece to be answered?

Once again, Gracie turned her heart to prayer. But she broke off suddenly as she came within view of the residence where the widowed Mrs. Cooper lived. There — in all his green, sneering glory — stood a lifesized Grinch!

Puzzled, Gracie walked closer. No snow clung to the figure — meaning what? That it had been placed there just this morning — or, for some unfathomable reason — wiped clean while everything else remained snow-littered?

Was this a new lawn decoration — purchased to replace the stolen Grinch? She frowned. What had Patsy said was broken? The arm? Examining both arms carefully, Gracie at first found no evidence of damage — but then, her nose so close she breathed steam on the figure — she saw a tiny line, where glue had been applied, the arm replaced.

She straightened. Who? Why?

She had just moved on when a car eased behind her. Turning, she waved at Herb Bower.

Climbing out, Willow Bend's highly capable police chief grinned a greeting. Then he pushed back his uniform cap and scratched his head. "What do you make of it, Gracie?"

She shrugged. "Maybe not stolen after all?"

"My thought, exactly. Some good Samaritan takes the broken things for mending, then brings them back as anonymously as he — or she — took them." He asked intently, "What's Uncle Miltie been up to recently?"

Gracie gasped. Such kindness did sound like her octogenarian uncle — but would he have been able to carry such a big piece by himself — considering that on sidewalks sometimes treacherous with snow he relied on his walker — or at least a cane.

Might it have been possible for him to be involved in a scheme like this, keeping her in the dark?

"You've been awfully busy," Herb said. "And — let's face it, your uncle can be pretty sneaky when he's in the mood."

They laughed together comfortably. Uncle Miltie was dear to both of them.

"I don't think so, Herb," Gracie said, reporting what Uncle Miltie had said earlier about his willingness to mend the Grinch.

"It's like this now all over town," Herb continued.

"Everything's been returned?"

"Every last piece, both reported and unreported. All fixed. And just in time for the judging. Tonight, isn't it?"

"Late." Gracie sighed. "Right after the cantata. It was the only space of time left." A bit of panic set in. When could she possibly get everything done? "I guess it's not under your jurisdiction to push Christmas a day or two later?"

He *hmmphed.* "Every other holiday's had its date changed, hasn't it?"

"Almost."

"You're always so busy, Gracie. How do

you do it? Especially this time of year. Well, maybe, come January, you'll have a chance to hibernate for a while."

She murmured agreement, but knew better.

He shook himself, sighing. "Guess I'd better examine the various scenes of the crimes. Make our mayor happy." He asked with a grin, "Want to go along, in case I need backup?"

She thanked him, but declined.

She knew she needed more time with the Lord.

Later that morning, Uncle Miltie accompanied her to the giant supermarket in Mason City, where they wheeled two carts loaded with plastic-bagged groceries to Fannie Mae's parking place. Gracie arrived first, and looked back to see Uncle Miltie struggling to manage both the cart and his walker, each of which was dragging in the slush.

"I'll make it!" he called, obviously reading her intention. "Don't worry!" he said, minutes later. And again, "Almost there."

Lord, a spirit of independence can be a wonderful thing, but this sweet man sometimes overdoes it, doesn't he?

Once they were finished loading, Gracie

insisted that she return both carts. That Uncle Miltie didn't offer a protest proved just how depleted his energy was.

For half of the trip home, he leaned back, eyes closed. Then, drawing a long breath, he straightened, cleared his throat and asked, "What do you make of those decorations being returned, Gracie? Any idea who's behind it?"

All she sensed — but it was hard to put it exactly into words — was that Herb Bower had been right when he mentioned sneakiness.

Sneaky, as it turned out, in a way that made the mystery just that much more mysterious. Sneaky wasn't usually equated with good deeds, after all.

Uncle Miltie was waiting for an answer.

"I have no idea," she said, slowing for a turn. "Do you?"

At first, he didn't answer. Then, to Gracie's surprise, he said, "You know, I might. I just might."

21

Scheduling the rehearsals for the cantata at the same time as pageant practice made for bedlam.

At one frustrating juncture, Barb threw up her hands in despair, and her baton took flight. Fortunately, no one was injured. Rocky — there to do a behind-the-scenes story — saw it coming and deflected it with his pad. *Clunk!*

Barb dropped her head into her hands, the children stilled — though only in temporary shock — and Maria, hands fluttering and skirts swishing, swept from the choir loft to flutter around the uninjured editor.

"Your head, my Rocco! Let me bathe it and make it strong — strong as you are. . . ."

"I'm okay."

But Maria looked doubtful at this.

"Honest!" Rocky insisted.

"You are certain?" She stroked, prodded and cooed.

Trying to wriggle free, Rocky threw Gracie a beseeching glance.

She was tempted to ignore it. The entire choir — Barb included — was obviously enjoying the encounter. Gracie wondered who was rooting for whom.

It actually didn't seem a bad idea to allow Rocky to squirm for a bit. It was when he mouthed, "Please," like Gooseberry's silent meow, employed only in desperate situations, that she could no longer leave her friend undefended.

Hurrying down the aisle, she placed her arm across Maria's tense shoulders. "Dear Maria, you're sweet to be concerned, but Rocky's safe for now — safe at least from flying missiles. Just now, I'm afraid he's in greater danger of suffocation!" Gently, she tugged Maria into the aisle.

"Suffocate!" Maria's eyes widened in alarm. Then she relaxed, chuckling. "*Ah, Gracia,* my friend, you make the joke." She waggled her finger. "But no. To hurt my Rocco? Never!"

As the two women moved companionably toward the choir loft, Gracie glanced back. Rocky was collapsed in his seat, looking paralyzed, as though he were a passenger shipwrecked on an island he was now afraid to leave.

■ ■ ■ ■

From that moment on, the dress rehearsal went more smoothly. There were still forgotten lines and erupting youthful horseplay, but, in the main, the tide had been turned.

Hurry, hurry! Leave your studies
In their tumbled disarray . . .
Charts and maps and figures jumbled —
Come, be quickly on your way!

"No, no no!" Barb protested, rapping her baton. "Work to find the rolling rhythm of camels traversing sand. Close your eyes — picture it! Their steady, onward motion. And always the haste! The haste! The urgency!

"Try it again," she commanded, with commendable calm.

Hurry, hurry! Join your comrades,
Moving through the bustling dark.
See the starbeam, like a signal —
Like a beacon — stream and spark!

"Better. Much, much better!" Gracie couldn't hear the words, but Barb's expression said everything.

The fear they must have felt! Lord, what

could it have been like? We, who board a plane so casually, with every expectation that in a few hours we will have traveled thousands of miles, how can we possibly imagine the perils and deprivations of that extraordinary journey?

"Well," Barb sighed, laying her baton carefully on the music stand. "What do you think, Gracie?"

"It's going to be fine!"

"You guarantee it?"

"Absolutely!" Gracie added, smiling, "Of course, in any poll there's a three to five percent margin of error."

Barb hugged her. "You're such a comfort! Thanks!"

"Remember, though, when the dress rehearsal goes poorly, the performance goes well."

Barb retorted, "Well, if that old saw holds true, we must be nearly ready for Carnegie Hall!"

22

The angels were angelic, the shepherds remembered their responsibilities, the wise men hurried as the bass section found the rhythm Barb had visualized. Herod — in rich robes that flared and glittered — portrayed the perfect combination of manic evil and paranoia.

The choir did Barb proud. Singing from shadows with only small flashlights for illumination, they underlined all the drama, pathos, fear, exultation — whatever mood played out in the action.

But the highlight of a wonderful performance came when Patsy took her place by the manger, where animals painted on cardboard and canvas were backed by recorded bleats, moos and neighs.

She had advanced somberly, soberly, on Joseph's arm — while the choir sang softly:

Pitter, patter, donkey's feet

Clatter down the busy street.
Ears that flip-flop, chasing flies
Hear a hundred market cries . . .

Methodically, innkeepers turned them
away — some angrily, others compassion-
ately — until at length they were led to the
stable by a bathrobe-clad teen holding a
lantern high.

Joseph — tired, concerned — thanked the
kind innkeeper, who withdrew with his
lantern light to tend more fortunate guests.

Carefully, Mary — Patsy — moved to the
manger, and was in the act of kneeling when
suddenly she gave a startled glad "Oh!" Her
hands flew to her face. "He's real!" She sank
to her knees, her folded hands extended
over the crib, her face uplifted. From the
choir area, Gracie could see a glint of tears
on the child's face.

Lord, what's happening? Obviously, to
Patsy, new significance had come. Gracie
divided her mind between praise and prayer
for Patsy and careful attention to her vocal
duties, while at the manger side, Patsy
cooed and patted, much as the original
Mary must have done.

It was traditional, at Eternal Hope, to close
the Christmas pageant by encircling the

sanctuary with everyone in attendance holding small candles. Once all other lights were extinguished, Barb struck the opening note, and the entire assemblage joined in a loving rendition of "Silent Night."

Estelle always fussed that somebody would become a human torch, the way the children flailed around — but so far no one had even become singed — so her advice — like Estelle herself — was taken lightly.

Poor Estelle, Gracie thought. The thought was still with her when Pastor Paul pronounced the benediction and the sanctuary lights were back on. On impulse, she suddenly asked, "Estelle, would you like to have Christmas dinner with us?"

When Uncle Miltie heard, she thought, he might threaten to go to the mission kitchen for Christmas dinner — and take Gooseberry with him, for the cat's well-being.

But also to her surprise, Estelle laid her hand on Gracie's elbow, saying simply, "Oh, Gracie! How precious you are!"

Any reply Gracie might have made was forestalled when Estelle answered, "I'd love to, Gracie."

Now in attendance, besides Uncle Miltie, Gracie's niece Carter and herself, would be Estelle, Rocky, Pastor Paul and the Searfosses. Marge was having Christmas dinner at

Pleasant Haven, where her mother now resided. Gracie was already mentally setting the table when a voice intruded on her thoughts.

"But I can't."

Gracie stopped in the act of removing her robe to regard Estelle, whose expression held unaccustomed softness.

"You can't join us for Christmas dinner?"

"Honestly, Gracie, do you need a hearing aid? No, I'm sorry but I have other plans."

Well, Gracie thought, Uncle Miltie would be relieved. Actually, he'd never need to learn about her rash invitation.

Estelle explained, "The Claytons have invited me!"

Gracie said nothing. She couldn't have if she'd had the words. But her heart was touched. Patsy's life hadn't been easy, yet her generosity of spirit had made her see past Estelle's crusty surface.

The problem was, Patsy herself hadn't been doing much smiling of late. Had Estelle's unhappiness somehow distracted the little girl from her own?

Estelle exclaimed, "She's so brave!"

"Yes, she is," Gracie agreed wholeheart-edly.

"Watching her," Estelle shook her head, "suddenly I feel ashamed to complain about anything! I can walk so easily, yet with her, every step's a struggle. Pain is her constant companion. How can I not learn from her example?"

One prayer answered, Lord, Gracie breathed thankfully. *Hallelujah!*

Humming, Estelle turned away to hang her robe. Then, over her shoulder she said, "The Claytons have even asked me to sing, after dinner. I've decided to do the solo Barb gave to —" she tightened her lips — "to that woman. What a travesty!"

Gracie knew she had to be honest. "I thought Maria was wonderful!"

Estelle shrugged. "It's a matter of the trained critical ear, I suppose."

As Gracie left the room, she wanted to tell the Lord that the job on Estelle apparently wasn't finished yet — but she didn't want to discourage Him — not with His Son's birthday so close.

On the way to the refreshments, Patsy approached fairly quivering with excitement.

"Hurry, Mrs. Parks! Hurry, hurry, hurry —"

Gracie had to smile.

"That does sound like the Wise Men song, doesn't it?" Patsy laughed. "I loved that song! I loved everything we did! But especially I love that God —" Her voice broke, and she tried again. "I love that He truly did answer my sheepskin!"

If it hadn't been for her walker, she would have danced, Gracie was sure. She reached to embrace the child, and felt her trembling. "Sit down, dear, and tell me all about it, won't you?" She was glad it was the Turner twins' night to serve refreshments and do cleanup; besides, later Gracie would be busy judging Christmas decorations.

They found folding chairs near the coatrack. Gracie saw Uncle Miltie and Rocky waiting for her, but she only gave them a little wave accompanied by a smile that said she'd be along in a few moments.

"Now, Patsy," she invited, when they were settled.

Patsy leaned forward. Her eyes danced. Her breath smelled of candy cane. " 'member I told you about the sheepskin?"

Gracie nodded.

" 'Cause I wanted to be sure — about God." She waited.

Gracie said, "I remember."

"But I didn't tell you what the sheepskin was."

"No." Did it truly matter, she wondered, when so obviously the child's happiness — and faith — were restored?

"It was that the baby would turn real."
Gracie frowned.

"The Christ Child! In the manger!" Patsy shook Gracie's arm. "Mrs. Parks, are you listening? We've always used a baby doll before — always! And we did this time, too — for practices, I mean. But tonight — in the manger — it was a real baby! Squirming and looking like it was going to cry — I couldn't believe it, at first!"

She sighed. "But you know how people try to explain away stuff in the Bible? Like say the miracles didn't happen — the water was just shallow where Jesus was walking, or all the bread and fishes didn't come from the little boy's basket and people were ashamed to be selfish and shared?"

Gracie struggled to contain her amusement. Little Patsy was the picture of indignation.

Patsy asked, "Well, you know what Mr. Gravino said, when I told him?" She patted the arm she had so recently shaken. "I would've told you first — I meant to! — but when you weren't there and I saw him . . ." She burst into giggles. "I just couldn't hold it in!"

Gracie hesitated before inquiring, "What did Roc — Mr. Gravino say?"

"He said that he saw Mrs. Harding take

the baby doll out and lay her cousin's baby in. They're visiting for Christmas, and her cousin said she'd love for her baby to be in the pageant — that's what Mr. Gravino said — and so Mrs. Harding went ahead, and just forgot to tell me."

She propped a hand on her knee and frankly glowered. "That's what he said!"

"Oh, my dear Patsy!"

"I know!" Patsy exulted. "Isn't it something? It doesn't matter who laid the baby there, it was God made them do it — 'cause I asked." Her voice lowered. " 'cause He wanted me to know He's real. It's like my very own miracle."

Gracie gathered the child into her arms. As she brushed her face against Patsy's she felt her tears mingle with the little girl's. But, suddenly, there was Uncle Miltie at her elbow, saying it was time to get going. They had all those decorations to judge.

23

Mayor Ritter decreed they should all ride together in his van.

Uncle Miltie muttered, "Like a royal coach!"

The middle seat had already been claimed by Sherry Ritter and an art teacher from the high school. With difficulty, Uncle Miltie crawled into the back with Les Twomley and Gracie.

"As a kid I always loved driving around bundled up in the car with my parents, figuring out which front yards, with all their decorations, were my favorites," Les said cheerfully. "This is just a way for us grown-ups to get to do the same thing!"

After the emotional high of the pageant and Patsy's declaration of restored faith, Gracie was thinking she needed to come down "off the mountain," when Uncle Miltie began a mini-barrage of in-van entertainment.

"Okay, try this," he said, clearing his throat. "Ever hear about the cranky puppy? His owner had to keep him in the whine cellar."

There was a chorus of soft groans.

"But, listen, I got another grape one!" He chortled. "It's really grape!" he repeated. "What did the shrink say to the stressed-out Chianti? Give up? You need to wine down!"

This time, Gracie groaned the loudest.

"Too rowdy back there!" Rocky called from the front, but Gracie was sure that given his druthers he'd choose even Uncle Miltie's corny jokes over Tom Ritter's pomposity.

Uncle Miltie said happily, "I guess he means I should put a cork in it!"

The van slowed to a stop.

"Pretty spectacular, right?" Tom Ritter asked them, pointing out the window. It was his own house he was admiring, however, and Gracie felt mutinous.

The house had been left to the Ritters by a distant aunt. No longer a simple Cape Cod, the buidling now sported two additional wings, several balconies, a portico and pillars. Only the Ritters referred to it as the mayoral mansion, but, to Gracie's mind, that was already two people too many.

The gutters had been strung with three strands of lights — red, white and blue. Huge lighted snowflakes filled each front window, and a scaffold atop the chimney supported a massive electric American flag, with a timer controlling its lights to simulate movement.

It was impossible to say anything that would satisfy Tom Ritter as completely as his own appreciation. But Gracie felt compelled to offer, "It's wonderfully bright, Tom. A . . . grand effect."

Sherry spoke up now. "We just thought you should see it, to get an idea of what's possible if you're truly creative. Kind of a standard to go by, really."

Satisfied now, Tom Ritter drove on.

Actually, Gracie enjoyed the several hours of judging. Her fellow Willow Benders had done themselves proud. They always did, even without a contest. She felt a warmth, the Christmas spirit, growing within her as they proceeded slowly, commenting on each display. Nor did it hurt that snow fell lazily, adding its special magic.

The Christmas lights and displays were often excessively gaudy but somehow always heartening. God's love and the gift of His son weren't about giant candy canes, Gracie knew, or reindeer glowing on rooftops, but her spirit, nonetheless, was entirely uplifted and gladdened by this simple pleasure.

Even if it was a way for people to show off, consuming too much electricity, she didn't care. Just like Les, she told herself, I feel as if I'm a little girl again, awed by the wonder of it all.

"I think we 'done good!' " Uncle Miltie assessed as he spooned peppermint stick ice cream into two bowls and vanilla into one. He dribbled chocolate sauce over two of them. "This stuff isn't good for cats," he apologized to Gooseberry, who didn't seem to mind at all that his treat was unadorned. Vanilla was his favorite flavor.

"What do you say, Gracie?"

"I'm glad we did it. I remember when El and I used to take Arlen and his little buddies out, all bundled in blankets and with thermoses of hot chocolate. The simple truth is, it's fun!"

When they were finished, the bowls rinsed and placed in the dishwasher, Uncle Miltie tilted back in his chair — so far that Gracie yearned to get behind him for fear he would tip.

"Don't you want to know?" he asked slyly.

She frowned. "Know . . . what?"

"Who I think it is."

"Who you think is what?"

"The decoration thief." He leaned forward, elbows on the table. His eyes fairly danced. "Well, I won't tell you. Not just yet. But I will let you help me set a trap."

Although there seemed no malice in his voice or expression, she reminded him, "He — whoever it is — mended and returned them."

He nodded. "Then can you think of anybody more deserving of a hearty Christmas thanks?"

24

"First off," he said, "do you have any old decorations we could break?"

Oh, dear, she considered, what do I have still stowed away? She thought of the Dickens figures Elmo had once cut out with his jigsaw and given to an artist friend for painting: Scrooge; Marley dragging his chain; the Cratchetts, Tiny Tim held triumphantly aloft.

But there was no way she could sacrifice one of those — no matter the quality of the repair. Nor could she allow damage to the huge wooden snowman Arlen had painted when he was nine.

"Well, there is . . ."

"Yes?" he prompted.

"I'll get it," she promised, "after you help me set up the others."

She had to admit the lights, the giant woven fir wreath, the wooden figurines — made by those she loved best — all looked wonderful. At least she thought so. At after one in the morning, standing outside in the still gently falling snow, she wasn't sure she could trust her judgment. In fact, she wasn't even sure whether she was awake or asleep.

"And now —" Uncle Miltie dusted his gloved hands in anticipation.

"Okay."

"It" was a five-foot-high Christmas tree. Many years earlier, El had helped her cut it out. But even his expert guidance hadn't prevented it from having some interesting jogs.

"Adds character," he had said, teasingly refusing to lend her his sander.

She had painted it a deep green, adding silver paint and pasted-on bits of old jewelry. It was a bit the worse for its long storage, and utterly expendable.

Uncle Miltie stroked his chin. "You certain, Gracie?" She was, but, nonetheless, she turned away to avoid the visual impact of the first blow. She couldn't, however, shut out the noise of splintering wood.

Propping it up, they allowed the broken top to fall naturally.

"Trap set," Uncle Miltie said in satisfaction, and led the way back into the house, and a very late bedtime.

■ ■ ■ ■

In the morning, the broken decoration was gone. How had Uncle Miltie known? Gracie wondered.

"No problem," he told her. "I'll keep watch tonight. We have a midnight rambler, is all. At home in the wee hours."

"Are you sure? What about the caroling? Will that affect anything?"

"I forgot the caroling." Sighing, he said, "I can go caroling next year, I guess."

Hugging him briefly as she passed, Gracie went for the coffee pot. "I have an idea."

He waited while she topped their cups.

"I remembered something last night that makes me wonder if I might know the . . . er . . . perpetrator, too. Otherwise known as our Christmas Good Samaritan, in the decorations division."

She leaned forward. "Suppose we compare notes, and each write down the name of the person who's come to mind."

Uncle Miltie nodded. Touching the lead of his pencil to his tongue, he wrote carefully. Folding their papers, they exchanged.

Both had written Trevel Landry.

Uncle Miltie exhaled sharply. "How?"

She described their confrontation. If there

hadn't been so much since to occupy her mind, she might have remembered before the broken decoration he'd been carrying.

"But who would ever dream that such a misanthrope could do good deeds?" she pondered aloud.

"I do," Uncle Miltie said simply. "And, with your own belief in human nature, and its power to redeem itself, I know you do, too."

It had happened, he told her, shortly after he'd moved in with her. "There were days," he said, "when I had to get away — even from you, Gracie, the pain was that bad."

She understood. "Missing Aunt Doris." She sighed. "I was the same, when I lost El. It was as though no one had ever gone through such a loss."

"I was getting around a bit better, back then, you'll remember. . . ."

He meant he had been using his cane more for insurance than necessity.

"But I just about played myself out that day, and was resting on a rock, and — tell the truth — feeling almost as if I wanted to die and join her."

Blinking back tears, Gracie took a sip of her coffee.

"Then Trevel Landry come along — him and two of those mongrels of his."

She grimaced at the memory of their snarls. "I hope they didn't scare you as much as they do me."

"One was almost at my throat," he confessed. "But Landry shouted him back."

She covered his hand with hers. "Go on."

"God wouldn't approved of what I was thinking." He shrugged. "Anyway, I kind of surprised the mutt, I think."

"Because you didn't show fear!"

"And there was Trevel, ready to shout me back, too. 'What you doin' here?' he growled at me. I began to think maybe the mutts were friendlier. 'This is private property.'

" 'I'm sorry,' I said, 'I didn't think it was.'

" 'Still ain't answered my question,' he shot back. 'Okay,' I told him, 'I'm grieving, is what I'm doing. I lost my wife a while back.' And then, he surprised me — he squatted down near me and touched my shoulder. 'Me, too. Me, too.' That's what he said." Uncle Miltie went for the coffee pot. "Want some?"

She offered her cup.

"He sent those dogs packing, and we went up to his cabin." He whistled. "A bit shabby, but tidy. We talked for a long time. I told him about Doris, and he told me about his almost-wife, and how he like to have died when he lost her. 'And them people,' he said, motioning towards town. 'The things they whispered — never had time for them after that. Still don't.' "

Uncle Miltie paused. "Gooseberry and me went back a few times, when you were real busy. Just to sit and not be alone —"

She caught his hand again.

"And he showed me his woodshop, out back — and a chair he'd mended." He spread his hands. "And that's it!"

She asked, "And you figured it out just from that?"

He blushed. "Not quite. I seen him the other day, when he was returning Marge's deer."

Gracie laughed. Somehow she'd suspected he might know more than he was letting on.

"He seen me, too. Just put his finger to his lips and rushed off."

25

Gracie was bundling up for caroling when Carter Stephens arrived. She hugged her aunt and Uncle Miltie with delight. Visiting Willow Bend from her home in Chicago was one of her favorite treats.

"I drove through snow the whole way," she said, "until I got within five miles of town. We'll have it here by morning, I think. I hope!" She gave them quick hugs, hurried up the stairway with her one small suitcase, and returned wearing a quilted jacket topped by a bright crimson shawl. She pulled a fleece cap over her blonde bob.

Before he waved them off, Uncle Miltie showed them the placard he'd planted where the Christmas tree cut-out had been. Affixed to the poster board was a red envelope.

"For Santa Claus?" Carter teased.

"Something like," he said — so it was left to Gracie to explain. After she'd told the story, she said, "And that's a note, thanking him and asking if he'd like to come to Christmas dinner."

Carter raised an eyebrow. "*Wow!* Trevel Landry should make an interesting addition!"

"I doubt if he'll come." Uncle Miltie wound a second wool scarf around his neck. "But we feel better for asking.

"What are we waiting for? Let's go sing!"

The night was beautiful. Still and sparkling, wintry Willow Bend was just the way Gracie liked it best. Except for summer, fall and spring, of course.

Maria, obviously uncomfortable from the cold, despite her many layers, bustled over to Gracie. "And where is my Rocco Gravino?" she asked, scanning the crowd.

"He's happy to listen. And, considering his voice, we're happy to have him as an onlooker. He makes even 'Jingle Bells' sound like it has sandpaper special effects, instead of sleighbells!"

Maria's disappointment was evident. On an impulse, Gracie invited her for Christmas dinner.

Maria hesitated. "I have much things to pack, Gracia, cara — since Chicago is only two weeks."

"So soon?"

Maria shrugged. "My sister, she is efficient."

"Rocky's going to be there —" Gracie began, not as enticement, but merely fact. But Maria immediately said, "Then I, too, will attend!" She placed both hands over her heart and whispered, "Ah, yes! One final embrace — forever!"

Gracie sighed inwardly. There was no getting around the fact that Maria, however sweet she really was, was far too dramatic.

So how many does that mean at the table, Gracie tried to figure out as they walked home. Within her mittens, she counted on her fingers. Uncle Miltie, Carter, the Searfosses, Rocky, herself, of course, Pastor Paul — now Maria and — if he chose to accept — Trevel Landry. Nine!

It was a good thing, actually, that Marge and Estelle were eating elsewhere.

When they got home, the message machine was blinking. Setting the kettle on to heat for hot chocolate, Gracie pushed the button — but they all three listened.

The first was from Arlen.

"Mom . . . Uncle Miltie . . . and Carter, too, if you're there yet — I wonder, could we change our minds here? Your grandson

199

seems to be on strike, Mom — says he doesn't care about Santa or presents or anything — which I sincerely doubt — but he insists all he wants is Gramma. And, of course, your peanut-butter chocolate chip cookies. Let me know if we can — or can't — come. Our turkey went back in the freezer. Elmo looked to make certain."

"Oh, my!" she exclaimed, thrilled. There was always a way to fit more people into her dining room. Love was the answer, and people's knees and elbows banging together were the least of her worries.

"Hop on that plane!" she told their answering machine. "Don't bother with sleeping bags! We're here waiting for you! We love you all!"

But the answering machine light, she realized, was still blinking with another message. She'd been so excited when she heard Arlen's voice, she'd not waited to listen to the second.

"Gracie, dear. . . ." At first, Gracie didn't recognize the sobbing voice as Sophie's. "Could you possibly come over? Tonight? It doesn't matter how late, I'll be up."

26

Sophie must have been watching out the window. No sooner had Gracie pulled up than the front door opened, shedding warm light onto the shining snow.

She was pale, obviously shaken, but no longer crying.

Why is it, Lord, that even small tragedies seem so much worse at Christmastime?

Of course, for Sophie and Abe, it wasn't Christmastime, it was Hanukkah. Still a time of celebration, of families gathering. . . .

Sophie drew Gracie to her in a hug that ignored accumulated snow. "I'm ready to share the whole story, dear friend, if you'll listen. But it may already be too late."

"Could I make us some tea?" Gracie asked.

Sophie shook her head. "If I postpone it, I'll lose my courage again. And I'm under an ultimatum."

Gracie started. "Abe?" Her friend had never seemed the ultimatum type.

"Not Abe. Sol." She explained hurriedly, "He . . . manages a sort of hotel for pets. When their owners have to be away."

"Your dogs are with him?"

Sophie nodded, on the verge of tears again. "They love him." She wailed, "Everyone loves Sol!"

What could Gracie answer? She chose, "He's a very fortunate man."

It had been, apparently, the wrong thing to say.

"Tell me about this Sol," Gracie urged.

"He's generous, soft-spoken —"

"And yet . . . he gives ultimatums?"

"Oh, Gracie, I don't blame him! He's been patient for so long."

Where was this going, Gracie wondered. Were the dogs giving Sol trouble? Had he threatened that if Sophie didn't return to Florida soon he'd put them out?

Was Sophie that wrapped up in her pets? If so, why hadn't she brought them along?

Sophie sniffled and wiped her eyes. "It's only I know what Abe would say."

Ah, Gracie thought, they were back to disappointing Abe.

And why would Abe care about the dogs?

Or — was this man — Sol — more interested in the dogs' owner? "Please tell me," Gracie urged. "That is, if you really want to talk about it."

"I don't want to." Sophie twisted a facial tissue beyond recognition. "But I have to." She straightened. "And the best way to say it is to . . . just say it. I love Sol, too."

"Oh." So Uncle Miltie, as it turned out, had been right all along. "But — love is a good thing, isn't it? Or —" she could have bitten her tongue! What if the love went in one direction only?"

"We love one another very much."

A new concern surfaced. "He's not —"

"His wife died many years ago."

"His children —"

"— think I'm wonderful," Sophie sighed. "They tell me if he doesn't ask me to marry him, they'll divorce him."

One by one, Sophie was quelling every possible objection Gracie could see. Tentatively she asked, "Is he younger than you?"

"Just a week older. Can you believe?" She was smiling through her tears.

Gracie drew a deep breath. "Is it that he's not . . . Jewish? Though I can't be sure, I think Abe wouldn't have a problem —"

"Solomon Levine?" Sophie asked, giggling. "Oh, yes, Gracie, he is Jewish!"

"Then —" Gracie spread her hands.

"What's the problem?"

Sophie's smile vanished. "He said — just an hour or so ago when he called — that he will wait no longer for my answer. That I must — within twenty-four hours — tell Abe about him. About us."

Lord, what am I missing here?

Perhaps he was poor — Abe would have no trouble; he himself had known poverty. Or maybe he had a criminal record — again, Abe was the most compassionate of men. "What's wrong with him?" she asked straightforwardly.

"With Sol?" Sophie's eyes widened. "Why, nothing! Sol is perfect!" She reached her hands to Gracie. "Don't you see? He's perfect, and I'm not! Abe will think me unworthy of Sol!"

Gracie didn't believe that for a moment. Abe made mock complaints about his sister, about her bossiness and trying to change his life, but the truth was, he adored her. Yet, for whatever reason, Sophie had this in her head, about Abe's holding her — his own sister — to some higher standard than he would a stranger.

But Sol was no stranger to Sophie. He loved her and Abe needed to see that, just as Sophie needed to stop anticipating her brother's reaction.

"Gracie . . . Gracie! You have an idea, don't you?"

"I do indeed. Get on the phone and call Sol. The three of you are invited to our house for Christmas dinner. Tell him to get a ticket and right on a plane as soon as he can. He can bring all the dogs, if need be — I'll feed them, too!

Sophie beamed. They hugged.

Fifteen at table! Lord, did I temporarily lose my mind?

After twelve people, all bets were off. She had to supplement her own place settings with some of her catering stock. But that was as it should be — the Lord did provide.

She glanced at the clock. It would be Christmas Day in less than an hour. Upstairs, her grandson lay asleep on a sturdy pallet at the foot of his parents' bed. Arlen and Wendy had begged to help — as had Carter — but she'd shooed them away fondly.

Uncle Miltie, however, had refused to be shooed.

Now, as she bustled about, he chided her. "Gracie, you'll kill yourself! Why can't we get some of those really heavyweight paper plates and bowls? They have them in beautiful Christmas patterns! We could probably find some Hanukkah ones, for Abe and Sophie — and her friend."

He said slyly, "I did tell you, didn't I, Gracie?"

She knew what he meant. "Yes, you told me."

She set him to work breaking bread for apple-walnut stuffing. When it was mixed and in the refrigerator, and when the turkey had been tested for the proper degree of defrosting, she ran down the rest of her checklist: five pies cooling, scenting the air with their mingled fragrances; potatoes peeled and soaking; green beans topped and tailed; yeast rolls lined on their pans for last-minute baking. The clock stood nearly at two, and so, finally, it was time for bed.

Yawning, Uncle Miltie headed for his room.

She didn't tell him that she'd be up again at four to set the turkey in the oven.

"Merry Christmas!" Abe hugged Gracie.

"Happy Hanukkah!" she returned. She hugged him back.

Sophie wore a wide, happy smile. "This is Sol. He made it, though I'm not sure how!"

"Happy Hanukkah," Gracie said. He was tall and had silvery hair, with a smile that matched Sophie's in width and pleasure.

Abe looked at them. "Even if he does live in Florida, he's a good man, and he has the good sense to care for my Sophie."

She beamed, and she and Sol linked arms.

With their arrival, everything was perfect. Well, nearly perfect. Uncle Miltie turned from the window, shrugging, his expression disappointed.

So Trevel Landry had decided not to come.

With an encouraging smile, Gracie put Uncle Miltie to work lifting casseroles from the oven: her special baked lima beans; a prize-winning zucchini casserole — with squash she had frozen last late summer; and yams with apple, brown sugar and butter. And, of course, the creamy mashed potatoes.

Anna Searfoss marveled, "You must have an elastic oven! And there was a turkey in there, too?"

"She's a wizard at organization! But you know that, Anna!"

Gracie laughed. "All us American moms have Thanksgiving and Christmas down pat!"

Suddenly little Elmo appeared, aiming straight at his grandmother for a hug.

Gracie wouldn't have traded this moment for anything in the world! And, anyway, her world was here.

Soon, the sounds of serving, eating and appreciative murmurs were interrupted only occasionally. But then came a knock on the door.

Gracie and Uncle Miltie exchanged glances. She nodded, and he eased from his place, slowly moving to welcome the latest guest.

Trevel Landry had arrived.

Now, truly, everything was perfect. Closing her eyes briefly, Gracie thanked the Lord, then rose to offer her hand to the new arrival, who shyly accepted it in his own.

"God bless us every one!" Arlen pronounced. And they all cheered.

Gracie's Wintertime Pesto Sauce

- ✓ 3 cups fresh spinach, leaves removed
- ✓ 4 cloves garlic
- ✓ 1 1/2 cups parsley, large stems removed
- ✓ 4 tablespoons grated Romano cheese
- ✓ 4 tablespoons grated Parmesan cheese
- ✓ 2 tablespoons chopped walnuts
- ✓ 2 tablespoons pine nuts
- ✓ 1 1/2 teaspoons dried basil leaves
- ✓ 2 tablespoons butter
- ✓ 8 tablespoons olive oil

Wash the spinach well and dry it. Then chop it coarsely. Peel and chop the garlic. Blend with remaining ingredients until smooth. Spoon over warm pasta and toss. Serve with buttered, lightly grilled chunks of Italian bread.

Gracie says, "Indiana winters mean there's no basil in the garden for those times when Uncle Miltie and I get tired of tomato-based sauce on our pasta. Substituting spinach and parsley works wonderfully, and it also gives extra zest to a macaroni salad when you add just a teaspoon or two. Like any pesto sauce, it freezes well, of course."

ABOUT THE AUTHOR

Evelyn Minshull joins the "Church Choir Mysteries" family from Mercer, Pennsylvania. She is the author of twenty-five books, including *Eve, Women of the Ark, Dinah* and *The Cornhusk Doll,* which won the Silver Angel Award and was a Gold Medallion Award finalist. Newly released is a picture book, *Eaglet's World.* Evelyn and her husband Fred live in their ranch-style home, which he built on three acres of former apple orchard and sheep pasture. They have three daughters, Valerie, Melanie and Robin, and three grandchildren, Micky, Jonathan and Benjamin.

The employees of Walker Large Print hope you have enjoyed this Large Print book. All our Large Print titles are designed for easy reading, and all our books are made to last. Other Walker Large Print books are available at your library, through selected bookstores, or directly from us.

For information about titles, please call:
   (800) 223-1244

To share your comments, please write:
   Publisher
   Walker Large Print
   295 Kennedy Memorial Drive
   Waterville, ME 04901

Guideposts magazine and the *Daily Guideposts* annual devotional book are available in large-print editions by contacting:
   Guideposts Customer Service
   39 Seminary Hill Road
   Carmel, NY 10512

or
   www. guideposts.org

or
   1-800-431-2344